SLATE MOUNTAIN

MARK LEYLAND

a division of Hodder Headline plc

All characters in this publication are fictitious
and any resemblance to real persons, living or dead,
is purely coincidental.

A Catalogue record for this book is available
from the British Library

ISBN 0 340 71607 X

Typeset by Avon Dataset Ltd, Bidford-on-Avon, Warks

Printed and bound in Great Britain by
Clays Ltd, St Ives plc

Hodder Children's Books
A division of Hodder Headline plc
338 Euston Road
London NW1 3BH

Acknowledgements

Thanks are due to so many people: my young test readers, Robert Leyland, Sarah and Nichola Rudolf, Beth Shedden and Neil and Heather Shepherd; the members of Bristol Fiction Writers, Paul Hinder, Simon Lake, Nick Walters and Sarah Wintle, as well as Christina Lake who was far away for this one but has always been here before. Thanks also to Susan Carter for the food and shelter, and to Dr Peter Yearwood, late of University of Jos, Nigeria, for helping with the historical background – any remaining errors are entirely down to me. I'm especially grateful to Fay Sampson who gave her time, experience and practical advice to help make this book a success. Finally, *Slate Mountain* is the culmination of a long journey. Debbie Johnson, late of Bristol University, has been with me all the way to provide unfailing help, support, enthusiasm and a belief sometimes greater than my own. For this, no thanks can be enough.

For Robert.
My fellow adventurer through many lands,
an unfailing source of stimulation,
and the best friend anyone could ever have.

1

'And where's your *daddy*, Madam Rosalind?' asked Gwyn Thomas.

Not *again*. Lunchtime and breaks were bad enough and Ros always tried to get away the minute school was over. But this time the tall dark-haired boy was standing right in her way.

'Get lost, Gwyn,' she told him. 'Just leave me alone.'

'Ooh, my lady!' Meriel was leaning on the low wall beside Gwyn. The boy was blocking the school gate, but Meriel was running things as always. She put her head on one side. 'Not until you tell us.'

If only she could – anything to get away from

them – but Ros didn't even know her father's name. Mum would never tell her. Oh, it was hopeless – no point trying to push her way past Gwyn – he was the biggest kid in Year 8 and had no problem with hitting girls. She stood still, said nothing. They'd soon get bored – this couldn't amuse even them for long, they'd said it all so many times before.

'And how's the pox, then?' grinned Meriel. 'Looks as bad as ever to me. You should see a doctor, Madam Rosalind.' She meant Ros's freckles, which still hadn't faded from her summer week in Spain. 'Why don't you go back to Bogbrush Hill where you caught it?' Meriel went on. 'Infect us all, you will.' She screwed up her small round face in disgust.

If only she wasn't here. If only she'd move house or emigrate or just disappear altogether. Short and plump and mousy, Meriel Davis was the one all the girls wanted to be friends with and none of the boys wanted to cross. Ros just wanted to strangle her – and she couldn't even bear to swat mosquitos.

'Not her fault, I expect,' said Gwyn pityingly. 'I expect she's a clone. Maybe she never had a daddy at all.'

'Hey, I know!' Meriel waved a hand and Gwyn

stepped aside at last. 'Perhaps Slate-head is like the Virgin Mary.'

They couldn't even say Mum's nickname without sneering – oh, just ignore it. Ros went out through the gate and turned left along the village street.

'Maybe we should bow down to Madam Rosalind every Sunday then.' Gwyn's rough voice drifted after her.

Now they couldn't see, Ros let the itching burning in her eyes dissolve into a few hot tears. Why did she always let them do this to her? After so many times, the same old things, why did it even matter?

In five minutes she was past the last house and on to the single-track road up to the moor. 'Don't worry, love, it'll get better,' Mum had told her, but they'd been here a month now and . . . Oh, it sometimes seemed as though there were no other one-parent kids in the whole of Llantri. There *were* none in Year 8, except for Danny Mould – and his father had died of cancer.

It was no good, Ros just didn't fit. They all had broad Welsh accents and taunted her for being posh. Back in Sussex *everyone* had ordinary brown hair like

Ros. Here their hair was almost black and there were no blue eyes, not a shadow of a freckle.

Ros wiped her cheeks with her sleeve, forced back the tears, trudged on. Mum had explained things to her years ago when she was six. Her father had been 'just a friend'. Once they knew Ros was coming, he and Mum had talked it over and decided not to see each other again. 'It isn't important,' Mum had explained. 'It's not the genes that matter, it's who you grow up with.' And it had never *been* important before – not to Ros anyway – not until they moved to Llantri. Mum had always wanted her to have a 'real dad', a man to grow up with. But she'd always been so busy with her job – had never had the time to settle down with anyone.

The thick dark mass of firs called Gam Plantation crowded close behind the half-ruined stone wall. Ros reached the seven-barred gate and glanced behind her. Doc was following again. She stopped. Why was she waiting? If she went on, he'd give up and turn back, like yesterday and the day before. Eventually he'd give up altogether. He wandered up the road towards her, like one of the Lost Boys in Peter Pan – small, rather plump, with round thick-rimmed glasses on his round pink face.

Behind him the town clustered on the valley-side like an old landslide. Town – that was a joke! There were no decent shops, no decent *anything*. It was a scabby little village and the comprehensive was only here because this village wasn't *quite* as little as some of the others. The kids came to school here from all over the place, but Doc lived in Llantri itself, down by the main road.

'What do you want, Doc?' she shouted.

He came on without answering. Doc's real name was Martin Evans and he was as Welsh as any of them. His problem was that he was small and looked funny and worked too hard at school. It must be even worse for Doc because he'd always lived here and *still* they wouldn't accept him. Then again, maybe it wasn't so bad because he'd never known anything else.

He stopped beside her but he didn't say anything.

'Go away, Doc,' said Ros. 'Go home.'

'You reading anything then?' he asked.

'A science fiction book.'

'Oh yes, what's that then? I read a lot of science fiction, I do.' Doc read a lot of everything.

'It's by someone called George R. Stewart. I think he's American.'

'It's not *Earth Abides*, is it?' It was. 'Have you got to the bit where—'

'Please Doc, I've only just started it. I don't *want* to know what happens.'

'Oh – no, well, I won't say anything then. But it's decent, mind, very good in fact.'

This was the only thing they talked about – books she was reading and he'd read. Doc had read *everything* – reading was all he ever did, apart from homework. He didn't watch telly, didn't play computer games, didn't do sport of any kind, showed no interest in the countryside, had no friends to hang around with.

But he *did* seem to remember every detail of everything he'd ever read. He *told* her every detail too – whenever she gave him the chance – but he didn't tell the stories very well, and what's the point in reading a book once you know what's going to happen?

'Go home,' she said again. 'Your mum will wonder where you are.'

'Oh *that's* all right,' he began. 'I told her—'

'Just go home.' Ros turned away and started up the hill again. When she looked back, he was still standing by the gate. Oh, why did he have to be a boy, and a Year 7, *and* such a midget? Back in Burgess Hill, Ros had been the second smallest in her class, but they were shorter here – apart from Gwyn, of course. Here she was about average, but she was a head taller than Doc, who must be the smallest kid in the school. If only they *could* be friends. If only he wasn't – well, Doc. But then, of course, he'd be friends with *them*.

How she hated this road. How she hated the slate-grey October sky. How she hated the moors, even though they were so beautiful with the heather in bloom.

Carreg Lwyd Cottage came into sight around the bend in the road. 'Beautiful location' it had said on the estate agent's sheet and it *was* quite pretty – in the photo, anyway. It was a mile and a half from school and the walk wasn't *that* bad, at least on the one day a week when it didn't rain. The cottage itself was fine inside – with all their stuff from Burgess Hill – but outside it was grim: dark weather-worn stone and even darker slate roof. It huddled at the roadside as though it was trying to shelter from the endless rain, while the moors piled up behind, as dark as coal-tips beneath the lead-grey sky. She hated it.

And how she hated tonight, the lonely evening stretching ahead of her, as empty as the moor itself. But she feared it ending, because once it ended, it would be time for bed, and every single night now she had the dream.

2

Ros was standing in the midst of moorland at the dead of night. She could see quite well because the moon was almost overhead and it was only a night or two past full.

They were coming towards her.

She was dressed in something long and white and filmy. Her feet were bare and whatever was under them was very knobbly – heather. *Wet* heather. The sky was clear now but it must have been raining.

Ros knew very well that this was a dream – *the* dream. She always knew – every time. She knew exactly what was going to happen, but she couldn't do a thing about it. And knowing this was a dream didn't make her any less afraid.

By now the first of them had covered half the distance towards her. It was a straggling procession, two wagons, each pulled by two heavy animals. The legs were rather horse-like but the feet seemed bigger than they should be and the heads . . . Knights had once dressed their horses in armour, so maybe these *were* horses, wearing some sort of funny-shaped armour.

Then there were the figures walking. Ros never got a chance to count them. By the time they were close enough it was always like this, heart hammering, breath coming quicker, shivers running down her arms and legs, even though she wasn't cold at all.

There were two kinds of figures: tall dark-coloured ones and smaller, paler ones. The small ones might be children. None of them ever came close enough for her to be sure. But the taller ones did – here was the first of them now, dressed in rough shirt and trousers made of something like sacking. The moon was behind him and the shirt came up over his head in a kind of hood, hiding the face in shadows. This was when the fear came, for she didn't *want* to see that face. Wanted desperately not to . . .

He came level with her, not five metres away, his movements ever so slightly jerky. If *only* he would walk on. Just like last night, just like every night, he stopped. Ros couldn't move, couldn't scream and there was only one escape – this was the moment when terror always woke her.

She clenched her teeth – felt pain. She'd bitten her tongue. He was turning towards her, and now the pain was swamped in horror. Because this time she didn't wake. This time she was going to *see* it.

As he turned he seemed to come closer without taking a step and the moonlight fell on him.

Ros screamed now, for there *was* no face. The sacking of his cowl came down in front, but it was dead flat, just as though half of his head, everything in front of the ears, had been sliced away.

The scream was over and *still* she hadn't woken. The faceless man turned away again and walked on. Ros found herself following him across the dripping moor. She couldn't turn to look behind her, but those noises – the rest of them must be following in procession as before.

She hadn't thought she could get any more scared, but now – surely something even worse was going to happen. What *could* be worse than that flat non-face?

There was a shape to her left – perhaps a low house with dark roof and walls. She followed the sack-man down into the black moon-shadows beside it, heard what could only be the striking of sack-covered knuckles on a wooden door.

If only nothing would happen. If only she could wake up. A strip of light appeared – along what must be the bottom of the door. There was the sound of a bolt being drawn and . . .

Now Ros understood. *This* was what she mustn't see – whatever was behind that door.

It began to open.

Ros screamed, jerked upright in the darkness, grabbed for the bedside lamp and knocked it off the table. Keep calm, keep calm, get the light on. She scrambled to the floor, pyjamas drenched in sweat, groped for it, found the base, then the switch, turned it on and set it back on the table.

She sat on the edge of the bed, shivering. She

couldn't sleep in this house again, whatever happened. Behind that dream-door . . . surely there was something in there that could really hurt her. She sat for a few minutes until her breathing slowed and the heartbeats stopped thudding in her ears.

Her bedroom was tiny – at the back of the house – nothing in here but a bed and a small wardrobe, but still there was barely room to stand up. The one small window was almost blocked by the moors. She'd always hated it, never came in here except to sleep, but there was nothing to be done – there was only one other bedroom and that was just as bad.

Ros forced herself to relax, lay back on the bed. She sighed. The dream had always been worse in this house, in this room. It had started about six months ago, when Mum was offered the Llantri job. At first it came only now and then, half-remembered, like an ordinary dream. As time passed it came more often, lasted longer, got more scary. Ros didn't tell anyone at first – after all, what harm can dreams do?

Then there was that blissful August week on the Costa del Sol and no dream at all. But the first night back, it started again and ever since . . .

Her tongue was sore, her fingers came away red

from touching it – she really *had* bitten herself. Oh, what was she going to do?

No point talking to Mum – she'd tried that last night. Mary Slater – Slate-head because of her name and her prematurely greying hair – was 36, but she'd never stayed in a job for more than two or three years, never really seemed to believe she was a good enough teacher. At Llantri, as before, she was doing all sorts of extra things in the evenings to make herself useful. She'd already taken charge of two societies and persuaded the Deputy Head to let her help with the timetable. And even when she was home she was always exhausted, always too busy with her own problems to even listen.

But Ros couldn't go back to sleep, not now, not in this cottage. Oh, what was the use? She gave up, went out into the hall, knocked on the other bedroom door. There was a sleepy noise, so she opened it and turned on the light.

'What is it, love?'

'That dream again.' She could be calm now. Perhaps that was part of the problem – she was always too calm. 'It was worse. It's worse every night.'

'Ros, you're bleeding. What's happened?'

'Bit my tongue in my sleep. Mum, that doesn't matter.'

'Oh, love! Come in a minute.' She lifted up the quilt, moved over to make room.

'I don't *want* to come in a minute. It's no good, Mum, we've got to talk about this properly. I just can't sleep in this house again – not ever!'

3

The geography lesson covered slate mining, once the most important industry round here. Thousands of tons of roofing slate had been sent all over Britain by rail and sea, as well as to Germany and other countries. That was about all Ros could remember – it was so hard to concentrate today, so hard to keep from thinking about tonight.

It was lunchtime now and obvious enough what was coming.

'Slater, isn't it?' said Meriel as soon as they were out of the classroom. 'Well, Madam Rosalind, these mountains are made out of the stuff. You should feel right at home.'

'Yes, right,' said Ros, 'you always make me feel *so* welcome.' It was stupid – could only make things worse, but with bedtime looming already like the most horrendous horror movie, it didn't seem that important any more.

Meriel said something sarcastic. She was quick and clever and vindictive – the *last* person to argue with.

'Oh, shut up the pair of you!' It was Gwyn, shoving his way out to the playground, pushing Meriel almost as hard as Ros.

He turned back to Ros and shouted, 'I don't know why you don't go back to where you came from and leave us all in peace, you stupid little madam!'

Ros couldn't keep from flinching but the expected punch didn't come. Gwyn just gave a snort of disgust, then turned and walked away.

'Who's in a stress today, then?' Meriel called after him. 'Got out the wrong side of your sty, did you?' She held up a finger to Gwyn, mouthed an obscenity at Ros, then went off in the other direction. She had to have the last word but she didn't want to feel Gwyn's fist any more than anyone else.

Ros hurried off too, before they could start on her again. She headed for the quietest corner of the playground and sat on the wall near the school gate. Fifteen minutes to lunchtime – they'd all get their chance then.

Mum was sending her to Dr Jones – Jones the Pill, everyone called him. She'd rung the surgery before school, managed to get a four o'clock appointment by saying it was an emergency. It *was* *something*. Mum had never taken the dream this seriously before – probably it was the bitten tongue. Ros hadn't been to Jones the Pill before but of course he wouldn't be able to do anything.

A white Nissan hatchback pulled up at the school gates and Doc got out. He must have missed the morning classes.

The car drove off and Gwyn came striding up to the smaller boy as soon as he came into the playground.

'Little scab! Why are you so late then?'

Doc didn't answer. His expression hardly ever changed, always set and serious. No matter what they did or said, he never answered, never showed how it must hurt.

The taller boy swore and punched Doc in the face – not all that hard but there was blood and . . .

If only she could help him, but what could she do?

'*Now* you'll tell me.'

What was *wrong* with Gwyn today? He was always a jerk but not usually this bad. He'd beaten up Jimmy Pritchard at morning break for no reason at all and been told off by Mrs Arnold for fidgeting in maths. In the end she'd sent him to the Head for swearing at her.

Doc said nothing. His hand was over his mouth and blood oozed between his fingers but still he stared back without expression.

Gwyn swore at him again, then turned and walked away.

Ros hurried over. 'Are you all right?'

Usually the small boy looked her right in the eyes. This time he stared at his shoes, mumbled something.

'Why are you so late? Let me look at that—'

'It's all right.' He took a hanky from his pocket, pressed it to his lip. Then he smiled. 'Never mind him. Look, Ros, have you got a minute? I have to talk to you, see.'

She smiled back. 'As long as you don't tell me what happens in *Earth Abides*!'

They went back to the playground wall and sat down.

Still not looking at her, Doc said, 'I know it's a funny question and all, but do you ever have *dreams*?'

As soon as she told him she was having the same dream every night, the little boy wouldn't let her say another word.

'I'm having a recurring dream too,' he explained. 'I wonder . . . We have to do this scientifically.' He pulled out a stub of a pencil and a pocket diary, ripped out a page, tore it in two and gave her half. 'Write down three things,' he said. 'Whatever you remember – from the dream, I mean.'

She thought about it. Non-face, perhaps? No, stick to ordinary words. She ended up with 'sacking', 'moor' and 'moon'. Doc made her hide her list, took the pencil and wrote his own.

'Now show me what you've got,' he said.

He'd written sack–cloth, horse–thing and moon. They went through the dreams in detail, found they were almost the same but not quite. They'd both seen the flat, sack-covered non-face for the first time last night, but the biggest difference was that Doc woke up as soon as he saw it and puked all over the bed. His mother had made a terrible fuss – apparently she made a terrible fuss about *everything* – and wouldn't let him come to school, even though he was fine by morning. Doc had never told his parents about the dream – still hadn't. He was worried how they might react.

As to *why* they were having the same dream or what they ought to do about it, Doc had no more idea than Ros.

Every doctor's surgery is basically the same. A doctor, a desk, three spare chairs, and one of those examining-trolley-things up against the wall. But back in Burgess Hill, the doctor had a computer terminal on her desk. Jones the Pill was in his fifties, with short dark hair and plastic-rimmed glasses and there was nothing here more high-tech than a stethoscope.

'Well, young lady, what seems to be the problem then?'

No point mentioning Doc's dream – Jones the Pill would think she was mad. She told him all about her own, leaving out the bitten tongue.

'Nothing to worry about at all.' He gave her one of those superior-grown-up smiles. 'At your age – well, you know very well, your body's going through all sorts of changes and that can lead to all sorts of funny things. If you get through with nothing worse than bad dreams you can think yourself lucky.'

Bad dreams. Not even nightmares. *You* try going to sleep in my bed tonight, Jones the Pill. *You* try finding out what's behind that door. Of course she didn't say anything.

'No need to worry though,' said the doctor. 'I'll give you something for it.' He wrote out a prescription. 'Take one of these each night at bedtime. You'll go all through the night without waking and you won't remember any dreams at all. Just for a week, mind. After that you'll sleep as right as rain without them.'

She collected the plastic tube of small pink tablets from the chemist, then set out on the trek home. Even if Doc *was* having the same dream as her, there had to be a chance that Jones the Pill was right. Tonight she'd try his pills and, if they didn't work, if she had the dream anyway . . . Well, this would be the last time she'd have it – in this house anyway.

4

Ros woke up in the middle of the night. Nice one, Jones the Pill! 'Go all through the night without waking.' 'Won't remember any dreams at all.' But hang on a minute – she *didn't* remember dreaming, so maybe the little pink tablet had done the trick after all.

It wasn't cloudy like last night. Moonlight streamed in through the window, making a little silver oblong on the carpet. Ros craned to see the moon – such a perfect white, so very bright, that awkward, rather ugly shape, not quite round, and not quite three-quarters either. It had been well up when she went to bed and now it must be at its highest. She couldn't have been asleep three hours.

Ros lay back, closed her eyes, and pulled the sheet over her head to block out the light. She didn't feel sleepy at all – great sleeping pills! She could always read another chapter of *Earth Abides*. Doc was right – it *was* good. But Ros didn't feel like reading. Time to think about her other problems. They might not be as easily sorted as the dream, but she'd put up with them for long enough – it was time to *do* something.

Right. She'd talk to Mum again tomorrow. Teachers are supposed to know about bullying. There must be a way to make her see what it was like.

Ros propped herself up on her elbows and stared out across the moonlit moor. Maybe she could stay with Becky? Yes – stay there in term-time and then come back here for the holidays. Becky Oldman was her best friend in Burgess Hill. Her parents had a huge house – Ros had slept over there lots of times – and they were really nice. They wouldn't mind, surely they wouldn't, and she could . . .

A movement! Up there against the skyline. An animal maybe – but what would be out on the moor in darkness? Bigger than a rabbit, for sure. Could be a sheep, but don't they sleep at night? A badger maybe, or a fox? It came again in the same place, then again. Now it was a shape and it was growing . . . Oh, it *couldn't* be!

Was this the dream again, but different? Had the tablet caused this? It was a man, walking across the moors directly towards the cottage, but the way he walked was slightly jerky, just like . . . This was ridiculous – who'd be out walking at two a.m?

Ros wanted to draw the curtains, put on the light, pretend she hadn't seen it. It *couldn't* be the dream because she knew quite well she was wide awake. Other movements now, other people walking, and something larger that might be a wagon drawn by not-quite horses. Ros jerked the curtains closed so sharply that one of them came loose, leaving the corner of the window exposed. She covered it up quickly. Don't put on the light – mustn't attract their attention!

Get Mum. If it was real – if Mum could see it too – she'd be bound to recognise Ros's description of her dream and call the police.

Ros ran to the other bedroom, didn't turn on the

light, shook the sleeping figure. 'Ssh, Mum. Come and look. There's someone out there.'

Of course Mum reached for the bedside lamp but Ros grabbed her hand. 'Don't put the light on. Come and look first.'

'Oh, Ros, I can't be up every night. I'm tired enough—'

'Just please come and look, just a minute, *please*!'

Ros led her through to her own bedroom, drew back the curtains. It was more or less as she'd expected – after all, it *couldn't* be real. 'I'm sorry,' she said. 'I was so sure . . . I'm sorry, I . . .'

There was a muffled knock at the front door and they both turned away from the window. Now Ros realised which door the sack-man had been knocking on in last night's dream.

'Don't answer it!' she cried.

'Don't answer? But it might be—'

'It's dangerous, Mum, in the middle of the night, out here!'

'But you said you saw someone. Maybe they're in trouble.' Mum went out into the hall and switched on the light.

'Please!' Ros darted past and stood with her back

to the front door. '*Please* don't,' she said. 'Call the police. Get them to come and see.'

'Stop being silly. I'll put the chain on.' Mum started to pull Ros out of the way.

Ros gave up defending the door, dashed into the living room and picked up the phone. She'd pushed the nine button three times before she realised there was no dial tone. She heard the bolt drawn back.

'Mum, the phone's dead. They must have cut the wires. *Please*!'

The yale lock clicked, followed by the softer sound of hinges.

'Open the door.' It was a man's voice, deep and muffled by something. 'I am the collector. You must let me in.'

5

Ros ran out of the living room and down the hall. The door was closed again but the chain was off and Mum's hand was on the knob of the yale lock. She turned it.

'Stop!' Ros threw herself at the door, banging an elbow on the hard wood. Something was pressing on the other side and she was shoved back. In he came – very thin, arms so long, they hung by his sides as if they were dead. Sacking everywhere, that flat non-face – Ros felt her head begin to spin and . . .

'I am the collector,' he repeated. No sign of lips moving – nowhere for lips to be. 'This one must be given up to me.' The voice was as cold, flat and grey as the slates on the roof. There was no question at all.

Ros tried to speak, to scream, but no sound would come. Mum stood staring at the sack-man and Ros grabbed her hand – why no horror, no fear, not even surprise? Why didn't she . . . But Mum just turned away, walked back towards her bedroom, her limp hand pulling loose from Ros's grasp.

'Come,' said the sack-man in his dead voice.

Ros dashed for the bathroom, the only place to lock herself in, but the sack-man jerked after her, forced the door wide before she could get behind it and grabbed her upper arm. His hand was thin and bony, but he was strong enough to drag her down the hall.

'Please let me go,' wailed Ros. 'Mum, help me!'

The sack-man pushed her through the front door and closed it. He took her round the side of the house and up on to the moor. Figures – like in the dream: the large ones and the small, the bigger, darker shapes. Ros was dragged along, bony fingers biting into her arm like teeth.

It was the pain of the grip that brought her back

at last – and the scuffing of heather stems against her bare feet. She'd been too afraid to shout or struggle, too afraid to think at all. How far had they come? Where were they going? Surely there was no village this way, only moorland, crossed by the main Caernarfon road, then the mountains. Why wasn't it colder with only pyjamas? There was no wind, but an October night should be colder than this.

The sack-man let her go. Better follow. The moon was bright, and other sack-men – she didn't want to look at them too closely now they were *real*, and so very close behind her. If she ran – oh, it was hopeless, there was nowhere to hide. Maybe the main road? Maybe there'd be traffic, even at this time?

The smaller figures *were* children, three of them in front of Ros. There was a tall girl with light brown hair dressed in something blue, and two boys who seemed to be wearing old-fashioned nightshirts. How come she'd never seen any of them at school? *All* the kids round here went to Llantri Comp.

Ros looked back. She couldn't see the wagons or the horse-things any better than she had in the dream. Suddenly someone grabbed her hand and she gave a yelp and tried to pull away.

'Don't worry. It's going to be all right. I'm sure it is.'

'Doc!' She looked down at him and he was smiling!

'When they came for me and I couldn't see you anywhere – well, I knew they'd have to go to your place after, didn't I?'

He was wearing blue striped pyjamas – just what she'd expect – and his black leather school lace-ups!

'Doc, you don't sleep in your shoes, do you?'

'No, but I was thinking, see, about us both having that dream and when you told me about that door opening – well, I thought I'd better be ready. Then I heard them knocking . . . I'd just got my shoes on when they came into the bedroom and pulled me out. Daddy just stood and watched them.'

'Doc, that was so clever of you!' She squeezed his hand. 'I wish I'd—'

'Do you want mine then?' he offered. 'You can have them if you like but I don't suppose they'll fit.'

She gave his hand another squeeze and they walked on across the moonlit moor. All was silent apart from the sound of feet tramping through the heather. The still air *was* too warm, thick with the peaty smell of the soil. None of this felt like a dream, but what else could it be? It must have been caused by Jones the Pill's little pink tablet.

On the other hand, it *was* totally weird, but was it really *impossible*? Lots of things never get explained: ghosts and poltergeists, UFOs seen by airline pilots. She'd never heard of anything like this, but if the sack-men made sure no-one ever saw them . . .

Hang on, though, Mum *must* have seen.

'How did your dad look?' Ros asked Doc. 'When they were in the house, I mean?'

'As though he was hypnotised. As though he didn't know that they were there. He just went off back to bed.'

Hypnotised! She'd seen that on telly. Suppose Mum didn't remember anything, just found her empty bed? And what had Ros told her: 'I'm never sleeping in this house again'? Mum would think she'd run away! *Everyone* would. Mum ought to know she wasn't brave enough, but how much time had she ever had to find out what a wimp her daughter was?

It *was* possible, then. And what about all those other kids who disappear? Everyone thinks they run away or get kidnapped. Everyone thinks they either find another life and never want to go back, or else die and the bodies are never found. There are stories in the paper every week. Could *this* be where they go?

Her feet were getting sore and oh, how much Doc's chubby little hand in hers meant now. Without that . . .

The girl in blue collapsed with a gasp – she must have fainted. How far had these children walked before they came for Ros? The nearest sack-man went to the fallen girl, picked her up, and carried her back along the line. Ros watched him disappear behind the dark shape of a wagon. Then he hurried forward, empty handed, to take his place again.

Perhaps *she* should pretend to faint. Then she could ride in the wagon too – but no, she mustn't get separated from Doc, whatever happened.

They walked for ages – much longer and she *would* collapse. What a wimp! They hadn't stopped anywhere, so all these kids had walked farther than she had. They'd kept going south – surely they had – but why hadn't they come to the main road? There was something ahead, a silver-black line, bisecting the moorland – a grassy track. They crossed it, went straight on – but wasn't that where the road should have been? The hills thrust up ahead, dark shadows blotting out the stars. By now they filled almost half the sky and moonlight showed the texture of a rocky slope, so steep it was almost a cliff.

As they reached it, the leading sack-man and the two boys vanished one by one, as though the earth had swallowed them.

6

There was a darker shape among the shadows – an opening in the hillside. The sack-man walked straight in, so Ros took a tighter grip on Doc's hand and followed.

It was dark in here, but the floor was flat and smooth. From ahead and behind came the shuffling of feet and the rustle of clothing. Ros went slowly, holding out a hand so she wouldn't bump into anything. After a minute someone lit a light behind them, bright enough to show the way ahead.

The passage sloped slightly downwards. It was at least four metres high and the walls were vertical and smooth as plaster. The four pale figures were visible ahead, walking steadily on. Was it big enough to get those wagon things inside? It didn't look like it and there was no sound of hooves or wheels behind them.

The stone floor was cold against her bare feet but it was better than the heather. There was a light ahead now too, no brighter than Venus in a moonless sky. If it was a torch, this passage must be very long and very straight. When they reached it they found a sack-man holding – well, definitely not a torch, anyway. It was a doughnut-shaped ring about twenty centimetres across, glowing like a fluorescent tube.

There was a junction here – tunnels leading off on both sides – and the sack-man pointed them left. In a few minutes there was another branch, another faceless one to show the way. This tunnel ended in a bare cave, not much bigger than her bedroom. There were two sack-men, the two boys in their odd nightshirts and a small pile of something in one corner. Two people followed them in, another sack-man and . . .

'Gwyn!' cried Ros.

'Doc!' said the boy. 'Madam Rosalind! What are you doing here?'

'I don't suppose we know any better than you do,' Doc replied. 'If you have any ideas, I'd like to hear them.'

Gwyn shook his head. 'Whatever it is, I've had about enough of it.'

One of the sack-men stepped forward. 'Remove all clothing,' said the flat voice. 'Put these on.' Another of them was laying out shapeless smocks of sacking from the pile in the corner. There were also undergarments and some kind of sandals.

Gwyn swore at them. '*You* wear it,' he said. 'More your style, isn't it?'

Two of the sack-men grabbed him by the arms. The third one put down his light and came around behind Gwyn, something small and bright in the palm of his hand. He pulled up the boy's pyjama top and pressed the thing against the middle of his back. Gwyn screamed, stopped struggling and slumped in their grip.

If only she could help, but Ros couldn't move at all. She glanced at the two strange boys but they looked just as afraid. The sack-men let Gwyn go and, thank goodness, he didn't seem too badly hurt.

'Remove all clothing,' repeated a faceless figure. 'Put these on.'

Now Gwyn was first to obey, stripping off his pyjama jacket at once. Ros was the only girl. There was no privacy and she just *couldn't*. But she didn't dare not. She picked up one of the smocks and a pair of pants, went to face into a corner of the chamber, and changed as quickly as she could. The cloth felt rough against her skin, but not as bad as ordinary sacking would be. She put on a pair of the sandals, plastic things with toe-straps, a bit like flip-flops.

The clothes seemed to come in only one size. Her own smock was a bit loose – not that bad a fit – but Doc's was like a tent flapping round his ankles, while Gwyn's barely reached his knees. The sandals were all the same too, a bit big for Ros, but the toe-strap would keep them in place.

The sack-men were waving and pointing. Ros followed them out of the cave, not taking Doc's hand again now Gwyn was here. Another walk, much farther than they'd come from the tunnel mouth and this time there was a sack-man with a light to lead the way and two more bringing up the rear. There were lots of junctions – this place was more complicated than a maze! At one of these another light was lit and one of the sack-men took the two strange boys off in another direction.

At last they halted at an opening in the right-hand wall of a long passageway. It was another cave through there. Inside were dim and distant lights which showed nothing, voices sounding as if they were miles away, and darkness, still and heavy, pressing down as though the place was vast as a cathedral.

'This is the work chamber,' said the sack-man. He turned away and walked back along the passage, leaving them to the darkness.

7

'All come here!' Someone was calling from across the chamber – was that a foreign accent?

They could try to go towards the lights. Ros looked at Gwyn and Doc who were just shadows now. Neither of them moved.

'Bring them please, Adam.' The same voice, deep but definitely female and – Swedish, perhaps?

There were three lights over there. One of them left the others, came bobbing along towards them, a boy about Ros's size holding one of the glowing rings. He had short black hair and light brown skin and he was smiling.

'Hi, I'm Adam Patel. Welcome to the best

work chamber in the mine. Come on.'

They kept close within the small pool of light as he led the way to a corner where a hut had been built in the angle of two rock walls. It was made of wooden planking with a sloping wooden roof. There was a door at this end, and three windows with no glass, spaced evenly along the longer wall. Children were sitting nearby in a circle on the floor, eating from brown plastic bowls with their fingers.

One of them picked up a lamp, twisted it somehow and it shone more brightly. She got up and came forward to meet them – this must be the one who had called across the chamber. Arms crossed and legs slightly apart, she frowned and eyed each of them up and down.

Back at Burgess Hill High there'd been a girl called Jane Corby who was five foot eight before her twelfth birthday. This girl was even taller and she'd make at least two Jane Corbys. She was about fifteen and her blonde hair hung down behind in a single braid, almost to her waist. She certainly *looked* Swedish, with pale skin, round rosy cheeks, wide eyes that were probably blue but looked almost purple in this weird light, and of course the corn-coloured hair.

'You speak English, all?' she asked at last.

'A bit better than you do by the sound of it,' Gwyn replied.

The frown deepened. 'I am Eyda,' she said. 'I am chamber boss. This is my crew. Adam.' She waved at the boy standing beside her, then moved around the circle, stopping behind two children, both with longish mid-brown hair and very pale faces. 'These are Edmund and Catherine.' The boy smiled, while the girl raised a white hand in greeting. They'd be about sixteen and fourteen.

Eyda moved on to a boy her own age who came to his feet – as tall as she was, but very slim. 'Quintus, my best cutter.' He nodded to them.

Next Eyda rested her fingers on the shoulder of a younger boy, short and stocky with dark hair and brows. 'Rhodri is last to come.'

'You are welcome here.' The boy flashed them a white smile.

'And this is Meee.' Eyda stopped beside a strange little creature, probably a girl, with dark, pocked skin and a bush of hair, matted like one huge dreadlock.

'Now,' said Eyda. 'Is my chamber. All do what I

say, when I say. Sit down now and I tell what you do here.'

Ros joined the circle and Doc followed, but Gwyn stayed where he was.

The girl faced him, hands on hips. 'Sit down, boy.'

Oh no! Ros had seen Gwyn look like this – only too often. Eyda was older and bigger but she was still a girl and Gwyn could be so vicious. He stared her in the eyes now.

'*You* sit down – stupid loud-mouthed cow!'

'Gwyn, don't!' shouted Ros – as if he'd listen to her.

Eyda smiled, tossed her lamp to Adam and stepped forward. Her fist caught Gwyn on the side of the head before he could move and he crumpled as though his legs were made of paper.

Ros had seen boys fighting, but this was *nothing* like a playground scrap. Thank goodness she was sitting down, or she'd probably have fallen herself. So savage – she swallowed hard and shook her head to clear a sudden blizzard of dark snowflakes from her eyes.

Gwyn struggled up to his hands and knees, white-faced and shaking. He managed to raise his head and gave the girl a mouthful of obscenity, every foul word of the playground in one acid gob of fury.

Eyda smiled again and Ros turned away this time, winced at the thud – she must have kicked him.

'Please stop! Please *don't*!' Ros looked back to see Gwyn doubled up, hands tight against his chest, eyes closed, not moving. The girl stood over him a moment. Then she turned and the smile was gone.

'Very well, you I tell now and,' she shrugged, 'this stupid one I must tell later. I am chamber boss. I say before: you do what I say, when I say. Here we work.' She waved a hand off into the darkness. 'Tomorrow I show you. Here we sleep.' The hut. 'And here we eat food. Other things,' she went on, 'over there is water for washing, also buckets. Others come to empty.'

That frightening smile returned. She came right up to stand over them. 'All is simple here. No-one makes trouble. Any makes trouble, you tell me and I fix. This is best chamber, best crew, highest output.'

She paused, stared at Doc, then at Ros, smiled again. 'Understand this – any don't work, I take them out and we don't see again. If any is hurt here, if any dies here – is not problem for me. Understand?'

8

Adam laughed. 'Come *on*, Eyda!' He turned to Ros. 'She wouldn't do those things – she's just trying to scare you.'

What she *had* done was bad enough, but Eyda grinned now – *nothing* like that other smile – went over to the boy and tousled his hair.

'Adam is clever. He speaks, even I must listen.'

'Come on,' said Adam, 'have some food. It's not bad.'

'Please,' said Ros, finding a voice at last, 'I think you've hurt him. Could someone . . .'

The tall girl's eyes were on her and she stumbled to a halt. Then Eyda sat down beside her, put an arm around her shoulders and Ros had to keep herself from shrinking away.

'This . . . this punishment – once is enough, I think. I think he is not too much a fool. I hope. Adam, please see him.'

Adam went over to the injured boy and tried to straighten him out but Gwyn curled tighter than a frightened hedgehog, groaning feebly. Eyda filled two bowls from what looked like a cooler-box and handed them to Ros and Doc. It was hot, a thick vegetable stew, quite tasty, but after seeing *that* Ros wasn't hungry.

'Good,' said Eyda, 'crew is complete.' She went to the two boys, dragged Gwyn upright, half-carried him to the circle and propped him in a sitting position, her arm around his shoulders now. 'Want food?'

The boy was still pale, still shaking but his eyes were open and he seemed to understand, because he shook his head. He leaned forward, resting his body against his knees.

'Good,' said Eyda again. 'You tell names.'

'I'm Ros Slater.'

'Doc,' said Doc. 'At least, that's what everyone calls me.'

Eyda looked at Gwyn, squeezed his shoulder. The boy was trying to speak, but no words came.

'His name is Gwyn,' said Doc, 'Gwyn Thomas. Please Eyda, can you tell us what's happening? Where are we and what are we doing here? How long do we have to stay, and what happens after?'

The tall girl's lips parted and her big eyes opened even wider. They were very blue. 'You stay here . . .' she hesitated, shrugged. 'Always stay. Is nowhere else.'

Always!

'Well, that is not quite true, is it Eyda?' said the older boy, Edmund. 'Tell them of Daffyd and the others.'

'Taken,' the girl said simply. 'You are replacements for John and Meg and Hugh.'

'Taken,' said Doc, 'but—'

'I come here,' Eyda shrugged, 'three thousand shifts—'

'She's been here about three years,' translated Adam.

'I come and Daffyd is boss. I don't speak this English, not so well – I don't understand. He thinks I want trouble, tries to punish, so . . .' She shrugged again. 'Then I am chamber boss. Soon learn this

47

English – good enough. Adam comes, helps me.'

'I never met Daffyd,' said Adam. 'I was *his* replacement.'

'But *where* has he gone?' asked Edmund. His hair was long and straight, his eyes brown and steady, but his voice was louder now and there was a definite tremor in it. Catherine – who must be his sister, they were so alike – was clutching his hand very tightly.

Eyda shrugged yet again. 'Is taken. That is all.'

'And it is always the oldest, is it not?' said Edmund.

Of course – *he* must be the oldest now.

Gwyn coughed – he was trying to speak. Eyda scooped a mug of water from a large bowl, brought it to his lips and the boy drank a little.

'Thanks.' His voice was no more than a croak. 'What *is* this place? Why are we here?'

Eyda frowned. 'This is mine. I show work tomorrow.'

'But *why*?' asked Ros. 'Why do we have to work in a mine?'

'This we do not speak. Soon, perhaps tomorrow, you see mountain. Work is no value – not for him, not until he shows—'

48

'Who?' cried Ros. 'Oh please, can't you tell us *anything*?'

'No-one understands,' said the taller girl. 'Tomorrow you see but I tell this now – here is safe. No-one hurts you here, not flatfaces, not anyone. I protect you. Now is sleeping shift. Adam, show them.'

Flatfaces – she could only mean the sack-men. That must be what they called them. Of course – everyone in here wore sacking, but surely no-one else *anywhere* had faces like that.

Ros followed the dark-haired boy into the hut, found ten narrow mattresses, one row of five against the rock wall at the back, another row beneath the windows. Three of the beds hadn't been used and they were made up with pink sheets, pressed and fresh. Each had a pillow and clean new garments like the ones they were wearing. All the others except Eyda and Gwyn had come into the hut and they all lay down at once. Ros and Doc took two of the unused beds, together at the far end on the window side.

The children were soon quiet but there were noises outside still: Eyda talking softly, Gwyn replying, someone moving around. Ros stood up to look out of the window and saw the two sitting together beside one of the lamps, Eyda's arm around the boy's shoulders as before. There were others coming and going, but it was too dark to see what they were doing.

Ros lay down again. Some of these names: Quintus, Rhodri and Meee – they were so weird. And what about those boys wearing the old-fashioned nightshirts? – they must have been taken to a different work chamber. But *no-one* wears nightshirts nowadays. This was crazier than everything else but she had to ask.

'Adam?'

'Yes?' He was in the bed almost opposite.

'It sounds silly, but – do they all come from different times?'

'Of course. Quintus is Roman, born near Bath. His father was posted with the Second Augusta Legion at Caerleon and decided to stay on. Edmund and Catherine were born in the reign of Henry VII, and Eyda's a Viking – at least, she came over with colonists from Norway round about 950. Rhodri's a bit later, I think, though I'm not too good on Welsh history. Meee doesn't talk so there's no way of knowing. I suppose she must be from prehistoric times – a cave girl, if you like.'

'What about you?' asked Ros.

'Shuttled up with my parents for a long weekend in 2051. I hope they got home OK.'

'So you can tell us about the future then!' cried Doc.

'Yes, for what it's worth, and you can tell these others. Past or future, it doesn't make much difference in here.'

'But how did they all get here?' asked Ros. 'I mean, I suppose they were kidnapped, like us, but time travel isn't possible, is it?'

'We don't have it in '51,' Adam replied, 'but they certainly have it here – or something like it. Look, we'd better get to sleep now – plenty of time for talking tomorrow.'

A few minutes later, Eyda came into the hut, her arm around Gwyn, who still looked shaky. She settled him in the empty bed and turned out the lights.

'Is not cold here,' she told them in the darkness. 'Is nothing here to fear. Sleep until food comes. Then is first shift.'

The mattress was hard but comfortable. The pillow

was firm and smelled of fresh laundry. That smell, so familiar, so ordinary . . . Tears had always come easily for Ros, but she hadn't even felt like crying since this weird adventure began. Now she thought of her own little bed, brought with them from Burgess Hill to Llantri. How stupid! – she hated Llantri, hated the cottage, hated that little cupboard of a bedroom, but the tears came now all right. If only she could be back there.

So tired, tired enough to sleep – but would she dream again tonight?

9

Ros awoke in darkness and remembered everything. It *couldn't* be real. And if it wasn't, if it had all been a dream, then this was her bedroom. She stretched out a hand towards the bedside table. Her fingertips found cloth, a sheet, the sheet covering Doc's mattress. No more wondering – you don't go to sleep and wake up again, all inside a dream.

The darkness was complete, the air cool and still. It would always be dark here, so what time was it now? And when had they arrived? – about breakfast time perhaps? Best to lie quietly until someone else got up – she mustn't do *anything* to annoy Eyda. The girl had been kind enough afterwards, but what she'd done to Gwyn . . .

There was a burning in Ros's eyes again. No way! – what good did stupid crying ever do? There were noises outside now, people moving around. Noises in here too and a light came on. No mistaking Eyda as she rose and went out of the hut. Her hair was loose, hanging round her back and shoulders like a golden tent, as light and clean as though it had just been washed. She was gone only a moment.

'Food is here,' she announced.

Everyone was stirring. Eyda returned to her own bed. With no sign of embarrassment, she pulled the sacking garment over her head and put on another – must be a clean one. The other kids were doing the same, but Ros just couldn't. Gwyn and Doc had probably seen her put this smock on, but there'd been no choice then. She took the clean one out into the darkness and changed there.

Soon everyone was outside and Eyda was ladling out the food, bright and fresh and smiling. She wasn't just pretty – with that cascade of golden hair, she could be a movie star.

Ros joined the circle, then groaned – halfway between glue and puke, so it must be porridge! There didn't even seem to be any sugar to take the taste away, but she hadn't eaten anything last night. She tried a spoonful – it *wasn't* porridge – well, it must be, but it didn't have that awful starchy taste. Ros finished before anyone else.

'Please, is there any more?'

Eyda grinned 'No-one is hungry here.' She took the lid off the pot and let Ros help herself. 'This food,' said Eyda shaking her head, 'is little meat. Once I have much meat.' For a moment she was far away, back in a world Ros could hardly dream of – 950 AD! Then she grinned again. 'Yet I think I am not wasting with this food.'

There was no washing up – at least, they didn't have to do it. So those kids last night must have taken the dirty dishes away. Eyda squatted beside one of the lamps, while Catherine sat down behind her to braid the waterfall of hair. The others came and went, getting washed and using the toilet pails. Then Eyda was on her feet, a lamp in her hand.

'New ones today,' she announced. 'I show chamber – only a minute. Every ninety shifts are new ring-lamps. These must last until then. All, come, stand here.' She waved a hand in front of her.

They did so, except little Meee who stayed where she was.

'Now,' said Eyda, 'no-one looks at ring-lamp.' She lifted it above her head and it blazed like a fragment of the sun.

The place was bigger than a football pitch! No, not *that* big, about ten metres from side to side and stretching ahead of them for more than twenty, to end in a sloping jumble of boulders and rocks.

'There is work-face,' said Eyda, 'where mining is done.'

There were pillars, about ten of them, supporting the roof and, over by the chamber entrance, another pile of rocks.

Eyda turned the lamp down again, plunging the far places back to darkness. Those rocks by the entrance were smaller and more regular than the mess at the work-face. The floor of the chamber had looked flat and fairly clean, the ceiling more like the roof of a cave. Ros had only seen it for a few seconds.

Eyda came around to stand in front of them. 'We work with small lights. Do you fear dark, small one?'

Doc was expressionless as always. 'Not really.'

'Some do. I come here and I never see such dark

before. I fear it – *then* I fear it. Is many shifts and I am chamber boss before I understand. This is our home. You are my family and you are safe. Now is work time. This chamber has highest output. Adam reads it on . . .'

'The notice board,' said the dark-skinned boy.

'Yes. Highest with old crew. With you three is same.'

'Just show us what to do then, Eyda.' Ros looked round sharply. Gwyn was never helpful, hardly ever pleasant. Now he was nodding and smiling like an idiot.

The tall girl didn't reply. She was looking round towards the chamber entrance. There were lights approaching – could be the washer-uppers, but Eyda had ignored them last night.

Sack-men – flatfaces rather – three of them, with two ring-lamps. The one in front came straight up to Ros.

'This one will come with me,' he said. 'He is hungry for her energy.'

10

'Go away!' said Eyda, not in the slightest awe of the flatfaces. 'I show work now,' she went on. 'Time is lost on shift. Come later.'

'He has ordered it,' said the flatface.

The tall girl scowled at him, turned to Ros. 'You must go with them.'

'Please, Eyda, you promised to look after us.'

'Is no harm – stupid flatfaces! You are back soon. Then I show. Do not delay,' she ordered the flatfaces.

'This one too, and this.' The flatface picked out Gwyn and Doc.

Eyda scowled and shook her head. 'Quickly, then.'

They followed the one with the light through the

labyrinth, perhaps the same tunnels they had walked before but there was no way to tell. At last there was light ahead, but it wasn't daylight, nor a ring-lamp. It was weird, colder and paler than a fluorescent tube and shining from above, perhaps down a shaft.

The flatface walked into the beam and – it was as though he'd vanished altogether. Ros stopped, felt a bony hand between her shoulder-blades, shoving her forward, then a tingling, as if all the hairs on her arms were standing up on end. At once she was through – and there was the flatface with his ring-lamp, leading on down the darkened passageway. Why hadn't she been able to see him from the other side?

Less than a hundred metres on, a new light shone ahead – could it really be daylight this time? These people never hurried – if only she could dash past the flatface and get out into the open air.

The passage ended in a flight of steps leading up to an entrance, high on a steep slope. The light which had seemed bright from in there was thick and murky with a brownish tinge. It must be heavily overcast. Ahead of them – it was too gloomy to see clearly – a slender bridge led straight out into space, spanning the gap between this hillside and a single jutting mountain of bare dark rock.

The flatface led on across the bridge but Ros turned back to the others. Gwyn looked as bewildered as she felt, but Doc was calm as ever.

'That mountain?' she asked the smaller boy. 'It's . . .'

'Not a mountain at all. More like some kind of pyramid, I think.'

Gwyn whistled, long and low. 'But it's *huge*!'

'Bigger than the Great Pyramid – much bigger,' said Doc, 'and look up there. It's flat on the top.'

He was right – it *was* a pyramid, with a square base like the ones in Egypt. She'd only seen those on telly, but Doc was right again – this must be much higher. She hurried after the flatface to get a closer look. The bridge ended in the middle of one of the faces and the surface wasn't smooth. The pyramid was made up of hundreds of stages, each about thirty centimetres high.

She'd read about the Egyptian pyramids – thousands of tons of stone, thousands of slaves taking years to build them. The exact numbers of tons and slaves and years were forgotten now, and anyway, this pyramid seemed rather slimmer and steeper.

They reached the end of the bridge and a narrow stair leading up the side of the pyramid.

'Slate,' said Doc.

Maybe it was. The stone looked almost black in this light, blocks of it all the same, like huge building bricks. They followed the flatface up steps so small and steep they might have been made for mountain goats. Ros lost count of them, but she reached the top without having to stop. So did Gwyn – who seemed fully recovered from last night – but they had to wait for Doc.

There were children working up here – still building the thing, obviously. The flat top of the pyramid must be at least fifty metres square, and it *wasn't* flat – over the far side a new stage was being built. Kids were setting blocks in place with the utmost care.

Doc arrived, red in the face and blowing hard, and they followed the flatface across the pyramid top. He came to an opening and plunged down into darkness – another stair, not as steep as the one outside, but with the same small steps, even more tiring going down. How was Doc going to manage?

Ros was about to wait and offer him a hand, when the stair came to an end. The flatface turned back under the stair and set off along a level passage, leading deep into the mountain's heart.

Dim light glowed ahead and they came to a room which must be right at the centre of the pyramid. It was small, roughly cube-shaped, and lit by a couple of ring-lamps, both turned down low. Too dim to see much, but was that a figure in the centre of the floor? – perhaps someone squatting down. Something odd about the shape . . .

Gwyn and Doc came in to stand beside Ros, and the figure began to grow. No, it was straightening up – those odd bulges at the front must have been knees sticking out like a frog's under some kind of cloak or robe. Now the creature was much taller than the flatfaces – it must be mostly legs – but the shape was hidden by the long loose garment.

'The children of the world shall come.' The voice was softer than an ice-cream shake and colder too, but underneath there was an edge, the thinnest razorblade. 'They shall give their energy to me.' The figure raised long arms above its head and the world exploded into blinding light.

11

Ros threw an arm up to cover her face. Squinting sideways it wasn't so bad, and gradually her eyes got used to the light, which was coming from the creature itself. From every thumb and finger-end of both hands, bright streamers went up to the roof, playing there like undying lightning.

Gwyn was cowering, head in hands, and even Doc seemed impressed. After a minute, the bright ribbons winked off one by one, leaving the figure in even greater gloom. Had his arms and fingers been very long and thin, or was that a trick of the weird lightning? She'd seen nothing clearly and she hadn't seen his face at all.

'All of you must understand,' said the soft, cold voice. 'You were brought here and yet I do not force you to work. Your energy must be freely given to build this.' He might have waved an arm around in the dimness. 'This is the shape of power, built of the strongest substance in this world. When my mountain is complete, then I will have the power to make the change so that others can follow me. Do you understand?'

'What change?' asked Gwyn. 'What are you talking about?'

'The change is the change. What was before, will not be. What will be after – it is not likely that you have the wit to understand, but you can see it. Go to the top of my mountain and look down. Then you will know something of the choice you have to make.'

The figure sank down again into its frog-like squat. This must mean the audience was over and the flatface at Ros's side was touching her arm, pointing back the way they'd come. Up on the tower top, he set off in the other direction. Lots of kids were working here, about the same ages as Eyda's chamber crew and all dressed the same. Some looked up as they passed, but no-one spoke and no-one smiled.

They were building the next level of the pyramid and there was no cement or mortar. The blocks were simply set in place, one beside another, yet the surface underfoot was smoother than a tiled floor, and the cracks between the blocks were almost invisible. On the edge of the pyramid top was a winch, a dozen children shoving on heavy handles to drag something up a ramp. Looking to right and left, there were other ramps, other winches, and the things being pulled up were sleds, loaded with the building blocks.

Then Ros noticed the plain below. At the foot of the pyramid it was bare desert, but farther off – so far down, so hard to see in this dim light – it seemed to be covered with a dark mist. Things were moving down there, lights, brighter than the soupy murk but not that bright, painted with the colours of sickness, yellow-brown, mouldy green, and the dirty orange of a sore that won't heal. The way they moved – there was no pattern to it and yet . . . This was the way she'd felt years ago on long car journeys. She was going to . . . She jerked away from the sight too late, doubled over and threw up on the surface of the pyramid top. Careful not to look down again, she hurried away from the edge, found Gwyn back there already.

'What is it? It's horrible, that is.' The boy was pale, looked as ill as Ros felt. He turned away from her.

Doc was still out there on the edge, staring down as though he was hypnotised. His legs buckled and he pitched forward. The nearest flatface must have been waiting for it. He grabbed Doc and hauled him back to stand beside the other two.

'Are you all right?' Ros asked.

'I think – I don't know really. I think I must have fainted – nearly fainted, anyway. What was it down there, do you think?'

'Well, it's not our dad's allotment, that's for sure,' said Gwyn.

Ros turned to him. He was trying for a joke, trying to be cool, but he didn't laugh and he was just as pale as before.

The flatface set off across the pyramid top towards the stair. Ros followed, glancing back to see children with mops and a bucket, already clearing up the mess she'd made – they must be used to that, too. Oh, none of it made any sense and who was going to explain it? Adam had to be the best bet. As soon as they got back, she'd . . .

There was something odd about the flatface in front of her – it wasn't the same one who'd brought them here. But how could she tell? They were all the same, tall and thin, all dressed the same. So what was different about this one? It was the shape: a little broader at the hips, a little narrower at the waist and shoulders, the same height as the others but surely . . . Ros went forward to walk alongside and the flatface didn't seem to mind her staring – no sign he even noticed.

The flat place where the face should be was just the same as every other she had seen, but on the chest were two slight swellings – this was a woman! Another wave of nausea washed over Ros – she'd never thought of these creatures as human, more like robots out of a science fiction book. If they were robots, wouldn't they all be the same? If these flatfaces could be male or female – and if the kids in the work chamber were 'taken' when they reached a certain age . . .

Better not to think about that, and anyway, they'd reached the stair. One stumble here and she'd fall

right to the bottom – no-one could survive that. All
the way down to the bridge Ros thought of nothing
but putting one foot ahead of the other on the
narrow shallow steps.

12

Back in the chamber someone was banging over at the workface – several people, by the sound of it. Eyda hurried over as soon as they arrived and led them to the face where Quintus was waiting.

'Are two jobs,' Eyda told them, 'cutters and carriers One of you must carry, others cut.'

'What do you do?' asked Gwyn.

'Carrier.'

'Oh, well, I can do that, then. You can show me how, can't you?'

A smile from Eyda and off they went, back towards the cavern entrance. Ros stared after them. Maybe

Gwyn *wasn't* completely recovered. Maybe that blow on the head . . .

Quintus was pulling at her arm. He picked up a metre-long metal rod with sharpened ends and a bulge the size of both her fists about a third of the way along. 'Drill rod.'

He clambered on to the top of a large boulder, a ring-lamp threaded on to his arm. After searching around for several minutes he pointed to a spot that looked exactly like every other bit of the thing, and started to make a hole by banging the drill rod down again and again.

'How do you get the rock down from the wall, Quintus?' asked Doc.

The Roman boy stopped working, shook his head.

Doc pointed at the jumble of boulders, then up at the end wall.

'Boom boom,' said Quintus. He must mean explosives of some kind. He handed the drill rod to Ros and it was as heavy as that old rusty sledgehammer she'd found in the garden shed in Sussex – easy enough to use though, once she got it balanced.

She could see everything from here. Doc and Quintus were working at the edge of the same boulder, hammering wedges into holes the Roman boy must have made earlier with the drill rod. Or maybe John and Meg and Hugh had made them – the children who were 'taken' yesterday. Ros shivered, though it wasn't cold at all.

Along at the far end of the workface, Adam, Edmund and Catherine were doing the same as she was, breaking up the bigger rocks, while the carriers, Eyda and Gwyn over here and Meee and Rhodri on the far side, were moving the pieces to the pile beside the chamber entrance.

Back and forth went the carriers, back and forth through the darkness, while Ros stood on her boulder, banging with the drill rod. It must be like this for worker ants, living beneath the earth, doing the same simple things in darkness for all their lives.

'Shift is over.' Eyda was delighted with progress and praised Quintus for teaching them so well – he probably didn't understand a word.

'Is time before second shift,' she said and led them

to the hut where the rest were waiting. 'All work hard and well.' She glanced at Gwyn who looked particularly smug. 'Until food comes, all do as you please.'

Not much chance of watching telly or reading the next chapter of *Earth Abides*, so . . .

'Some do exercise,' Eyda went on. 'Keep strong. After second shift we talk, sing, play games – I show you then. Now I run. Also are weights, also other exercise Adam shows us.'

Ros was watching Gwyn, just waiting for it.

'Can I run with you, Eyda?'

The tall girl smiled, picked up one of the ring-lamps and off they jogged around the chamber.

Ros turned to Adam. 'You said I could ask about – you know, everything.'

He smiled. 'OK. Rhodri, can you show Doc—'

'Oh no, I'm not missing this,' said the smaller boy.

Adam led the way into the hut – was this so Eyda wouldn't overhear as she ran by? They sat down, Adam on his own bed, the other two facing him on the end of Doc's.

'It's about – you know, what we saw this morning.'

'Of course.' Adam smiled again. 'I don't think—'

'Hang on a minute,' said Doc. 'What if Eyda finds out – that we're talking about this, I mean? She said—'

'It's OK,' said Adam. 'I've told you – Eyda's fine. What she said, before sleeping shift – *she* won't talk about these things but the rest of us can say what we like, no problem.'

'Well, I don't understand any of it,' said Ros. 'Why are we building that thing? And who's that weird man? – if he even *is* a man.'

'I've been here . . .' Adam began. 'Well, perhaps I should have been making scratches on the wall – it's so hard to keep count of days. Anyway, I've been here eighteen months, as far as I can tell. I haven't seen any more than you have and most people are like Eyda – they won't talk about it. I have some ideas but . . .' He shook his head. 'The one thing I'm sure of, that person we saw – at least, I hardly saw him at all – but whoever he is, he's collecting energy. When he has enough, when his mountain is complete, then . . . Well, he said he's going to change the world to . . . Oh, I don't know. Did you see, down below . . .'

'We saw it,' said Doc. 'Too right we saw it, but what *was* it?'

'I'm not sure, but there's something else I know. I always talk to every kid I meet, the ones who bring the food and the washing water, the ones who take the slate, everyone, hundreds by now. The first thing I ask is when they come from. How about you two?'

'1998.'

'Right, anyway, there are kids here from every age, back to the Romans and before, but I've never found one from a later time than myself. Whatever that guy in the slate mountain is doing, it looks as though 2051 is when he'll do it.'

'But if that's right,' said Ros, 'the mountain won't be finished for more than fifty years.'

'For who?' asked Doc.

'What?'

'For your mum and my parents — for them it's fifty years all right — but what about Adam? He's been here eighteen months now, so if we reckon the way you say, Ros, for his parents it would already have happened.'

'What's important,' said Adam slowly, 'it *must* be

how long *we* have – here I mean. After all, we're building the thing.'

'Maybe we can work that out,' said Doc. 'When you went to the mountain, Adam, the top was a square – you know, where the building was going on.'

The dark-haired boy nodded.

'Do you remember how big it was?'

'Yes – well, roughly. The blocks they're using are about half a metre square. There were at least three hundred along each side and the level was about three quarters finished.'

'I counted the blocks today,' said Doc. 'A hundred and sixteen.'

There must be a way of working out the speed at which the thing was growing, then.

'It's a regular pyramid,' said Ros, 'so – is there some way to work out the height?'

'It's not the height that's important,' said Doc. 'It's the volume. If the thing's being built at a constant rate—'

'Yuk,' said Adam, 'I hate geometry. What's the formula for the volume of a pyramid anyway?'

'A third the area of the base times the height.' Doc didn't even hesitate.

'Well, then,' Adam went on, 'if we can work out the height – both eighteen months ago and now – then we can get the volumes and—'

'It's easier than that even,' Doc interrupted. 'The height is in proportion to the side of the base and it all cancels out, you see.'

Ros sighed. If only she did, but she'd always been rubbish at maths. Doc was obviously a genius at this – no surprise there – and Adam seemed just as smart as Eyda said. Best leave them to it.

After a while they agreed that the volume was proportional to the cube of the side of the base – something like that, anyway. Now they were very quiet, both calculating hard.

'OK, I've got it,' said Doc.

The other boy made a face.

'Don't say anything, Adam, just tell me when you've finished.'

Minutes passed. 'That can't be right!' said Adam. 'If I had my D-link, this would take about three seconds. I'll have to start again.'

'No. We'll each whisper to Ros.' Must be Doc's 'scientific' approach again. 'If the answers are different, we can both go over it again.'

She put an ear to Doc's lips.

'Less than two weeks,' he said. 'No point trying to be more accurate than that.'

13

No way! That huge flat area and less than two weeks to build it up to a point? Adam came over to whisper in the other ear.

'Ten days. I couldn't do the decimals in my head, so it's just approximate.'

Ros sighed. 'Ten days,' she told them. 'It *must* be wrong but – never mind that, what are we going to *do* about it?'

Adam's eyes widened. Why so surprised? – *he'd* just told her. Doc showed nothing as usual, and neither of them said anything.

'OK,' said Ros after a minute. 'Do we have any idea who that person is? Could he be . . .' She stopped. Could *she* be about to ask such a stupid question? After what had happened though, maybe it wasn't that stupid. 'Could he be an alien? If he is, then he could be from another world – somewhere completely different. What we saw from the pyramid top – maybe he wants to change this world to be like his own, so that—'

'What he said though: the children of the world and our energy having to be freely given and that,' said Doc. 'It sounds more like magic to me. Merlin was from Wales, you know.'

'Doc!' He was the last person to start talking about wizards.

'It doesn't matter,' said Adam. 'There really isn't any difference.'

'What! Merlin's from another planet?' cried Doc.

'It doesn't matter either way. The point is—'

'What about the pyramid?' Ros interrupted. 'Why slate?'

'You're from '98,' said Adam. 'So you don't know about residual life energy, do you? It wasn't discovered till – 2004, I think. You had problems back then, didn't you? – pollution from burning oil and coal, nuclear accidents like Chernobyl and—'

'Yes, we know all about that,' said Doc.

'Right, well they discovered a new type of energy. It's all to do with – well, in the old days life energy was like superstition, ghosts and spirits and—'

'Are you telling us that ghosts are a form of energy?' asked Doc. For once he seemed almost agitated.

'Probably, but that's not the point. Everything alive contains a huge amount of energy – it's in the life process itself. They found that any rock made up of things that were once alive: limestone, coal, all sorts of things – part of that energy remains, and as the rock is formed, it's concentrated. Slate is one of the best sources – the energy gets concentrated twice. The original rock weathers down and turns to mud and then—'

'How do you get at this energy?' asked Ros. 'How will *he* do it?'

'I don't know. We have generator stations using limestone – quite small, nothing like that mountain. I've no idea how they work.'

'Is it possible,' Doc's face was creased with concentration, 'like critical mass, you know, in a nuclear power station – when there's enough slate, if the shape and size are just exactly right, the energy will release itself?'

'I don't think it's radiation, so that doesn't make sense, does it?' Adam shook his head. 'One thing we've learned is that there are always things science doesn't understand. That's what I was trying to explain before – it doesn't matter whether that guy is a wizard or an alien with more advanced science. The two things are the same. I don't see how your idea of critical mass can be right, Doc, but that doesn't mean it's wrong.

'I think you were right before, though, Ros. Whoever he is and wherever he's from, he's a colonist – nothing else makes any kind of sense. He wants to change our world – I don't know, so that his own people can live here, I suppose, though that horrible mess at the bottom of the pyramid looks more like—'

Adam broke off as Eyda came into the hut, flushed and grinning, with Gwyn half a step behind, breathing hard and dripping sweat. The girl looked so radiant – something about the strength of her sweat-damp limbs and the warmth of her smile – Ros just couldn't stop herself.

'Eyda,' she cried. 'We have to do something. The

slate mountain will be finished in about ten days – thirty shifts, I mean – and then – oh, I think the whole world will be destroyed!'

Adam's eyes widened again. He reached a hand towards Ros's arm, stopped halfway. Eyda seemed surprised too, but only for a second. Then she laughed.

'That cannot be,' she said. 'Redbeard does not permit. If you are right, then Mjollnir smites that one and his mountain is broken to rubble.'

'Redbeard?' asked Ros.

'Thor,' translated Adam. 'Eyda believes in the old Norse gods.'

The tall girl seemed delighted. 'I tell you tale of Mokkurkalfi – the Mist Calf.' She sat down on one of the beds and started into a really weird story about some giants who built a clay man, taller than Mount Everest, and sent him to attack the Norse gods. The monster proved rather feeble and, in the end, was defeated not by Redbeard himself, but by one of his servants, an ordinary man named Thialfi. 'Mist Calf is far bigger than Slate Mountain,' said Eyda, 'yet he is destroyed. If there is need, Slate Mountain also is destroyed.'

'Yes, OK,' said Ros. 'We have religious people too and they have a saying—'

'Yes, Adam tells me – are Christians. In my time all English and even some Norsemen – mostly southerners – these are Christians, too.'

'Anyway,' said Ros, 'the Christians say that God helps those who help themselves. Maybe Thor could work through you to get what he wants. After all—'

Eyda's laughter cut her off. 'Redbeard has Mjollnir. Hammer is thrown, never misses – one blow shatters Slate Mountain to dust. What need for children to do Redbeard's work?'

What a way to think – from Eyda, of all people!

'But God didn't stop the Nazi holocaust,' said Ros. Eyda wouldn't know about that, though, and Ros knew nothing about Viking history. 'Oh, there must be *something*, Eyda, some dreadful thing you know about, something Thor might have stopped, but didn't.'

The blonde girl's face darkened and she smiled. Suddenly Ros's heart was thumping and her chest was tight because it was *that* smile. What had she said now?

Eyda's fists were clenched to something harder

than stone. Then they relaxed. 'Yes,' she said, cold as a Norwegian glacier, 'I know such things. I *see* such things. Men must help themselves, yet you speak of destruction of Midgard—'

'That's the name for our world,' put in Adam.

'—This, Redbeard does not permit. He needs no help from children. Speak no more of this.' She stood up, still with a shadow on her brow.

Gwyn got up at once. 'Eyda is right,' he declared. 'We won't have any more of this talk, see.' And he followed her out of the hut. Good grief, had he even accepted the Norse gods because Eyda did?

'Adam,' cried Ros, 'we have to do something! You know her better.'

But Adam wouldn't meet her eyes. He looked away, shook his head, got up and went after the other two.

The food was especially good tonight, a thick stew with lumps of something – not meat, but whatever it was it was delicious. Ros almost choked on her mouthful as Rhodri swaggered round the circle, doing his impression of Brother David, the fattest of the monks in the monastery where he'd been educated. Rhodri was so ridiculous, so funny, and really quite clever. He spoke brilliant Latin and he was the only one who could communicate with Quintus, who spoke nothing else.

The Roman boy was laughing too. He shouted something, but Rhodri's reply was interrupted by a noise from the chamber entrance – banging, footsteps running.

Ros looked over and there were two lamps, people coming in.

'All wait here.' Eyda jumped to her feet, set off towards the disturbance. Gwyn grabbed a ring-lamp and followed, so Ros went too.

'What is this?' Eyda's voice. 'Why in my chamber? Why?'

Ros arrived to find two flatfaces with lamps. Eyda actually had hold of one of them by the arm, was shouting right into the flat non-face.

The other one replied. 'New worker – runaway.' He pointed off into the darkness by the workface. The hand he was pointing with held a pain button – a small metal disk like the one they'd used to punish Gwyn that time.

'So?' said Eyda. 'Is *my* chamber. Stupid flatfaces!

Wait here.' She released the man, scowled at Ros and Gwyn, repeated, 'All wait here,' and strode off into the darkness. The sack-clad intruders stayed where they were.

A minute passed. Then there was a scuffling noise, a sharp cry, the sound of falling stones. Another minute and Eyda emerged from the darkness, marching a tall slim black boy in front of her, one arm tight around his throat, the other twisting an arm up his back.

'Stupid flatfaces,' she repeated, letting go of the boy. 'Why let him come here? Go. Get out.'

The two grasped the boy and dragged him away.

'Why did you . . .' Ros began. 'Eyda, he was trying to get away from them!'

The Norse girl turned to face her. 'Of course. So?'

'You *helped* them! Why?'

'Helped flatfaces!' Eyda gave a short laugh with no humour in it. 'Is my chamber, my problem, I tell you before. He should not come here.'

'They've only just brought him to the mine. How could he know—' Ros was shouting now, but Eyda stretched out a hand, and took a firm grip on her arm.

'Hey, what is better – I fetch him, or them, with pain buttons? Stupid flatfaces in *my* chamber.'

This was what was important to Eyda, the intrusion, the invasion of her territory, not what would happen to the poor boy. It was useless to argue, but Ros just couldn't stop herself.

'That's not the point. He was . . .' She trailed off as she saw Eyda's lips tighten again.

'I say all stay by hut, Ros. Why don't you stay?' She glanced round at Gwyn, standing at her shoulder as usual. 'And *you*—'

'Sorry, Eyda. Just wanted to see if I could help.'

'Yes.' She frowned, turned back. Blue eyes, very cold now, stared into Ros's eyes. 'But *you* don't help me, do you, Ros?'

14

The grip on Ros's arm was almost painful.

Then Eyda sighed. 'I think . . .' She stopped, her frown deepened a moment, then her face cleared. 'Thing like this – don't happen, not here, not unless stupid flatfaces . . . Anyway, thing like this, you do as I tell you, Ros. Understand?'

'Yes.' Eyda's grip was fiercer still and there was nothing else to say.

'Good. Eat now. Finish meal.' The Norse girl set off towards the hut with Gwyn in tow.

Ros couldn't move for a minute, then found her legs unsteady when she tried. Back in the circle at last, her hands were shaking. The others were talking and laughing as though nothing had happened, but Ros couldn't make herself join in. However good the food tonight, she had no appetite left.

That poor boy must have been taken from his home today. So brave – brave enough to try to run. Why had *Ros* never thought of running away? – not when they were being brought here and never since. It would be easy to pretend to go to the toilet pails, sneak out of the chamber – but she'd never find her way out through the labyrinth, so there was no point. But why had she never even *thought* about it?

As for Eyda, most of the time she was fine, but that frightening violence always seemed so close to the surface. No point blaming Eyda now for doing her job – the only one to blame here was Ros herself. Eight more days and the slate mountain would be complete. Two whole days had passed since the boys did their calculation and she'd done *nothing*. She'd settled into this little community, good food, good company. The work ought to be boring – had seemed really tedious at first – but now, somehow, it was fine. It must have been like this for Adam and all the rest – settling in so quickly and just making the best of things.

Well, it wasn't enough. Whatever Eyda said, the time had come to *do* something. No way was Ros going to wait any longer.

The hopping game was played in a five metre circle scratched on the chamber floor. Meee and Rhodri were ready to begin, each balanced on one leg with arms folded. The idea was to hop into the other person and knock them out of the circle or make them put both feet down – a bit like sumo wrestling. No-one could last more than a few seconds with Eyda, but these two – the shortest apart from Doc – were better than anyone else, even Gwyn, and you could never tell which of them would win. It must help to be short, and they were both stocky and strong, like mini gorillas.

The others sat around the edge. The girls always shouted for Meee but the boys were cheering now as Rhodri drove the tangle-haired girl back to the circle edge. Meee leapt aside like an acrobat, almost sending the boy stumbling out of bounds.

Ros would just as soon support Rhodri, for the mediaeval Welsh boy was always friendly and cheerful, and so interesting to talk to. He'd been really well educated at the monastery – had lots of funny tales about it too – but the place hadn't suited him and he'd run away, just before being brought here.

In the circle the two squared up again. Then Meee lowered her head like a bull and took a leap forward. If she'd missed she'd have fallen for sure, but her head caught Rhodri in the stomach. It looked a stunning impact but neither of them went down. Rhodri was winded, trying to hop backwards out of range. The girl repeated her attack, caught him a glancing blow with her shoulder and sent him spinning over while she hopped on, right out of the circle.

'Meee is winner!' shouted Eyda. 'Rhodri is first down.'

The boy was laughing, rubbing at a scraped knee. 'So clever, Meee!' he said. 'Always you find something new.'

These games of strength and skill were the only signs of cleverness the little dark girl ever showed. At work, she and Rhodri moved just as much slate as Eyda and Gwyn. She ate with the rest, slept with the rest, but made no effort to talk to anyone.

And maybe Meee had it right. What good did

talking do? Since that boy had run into the chamber, Ros had tried everyone. Adam was friendly as before, but he wouldn't talk about the slate mountain at all now – whatever he said he *must* be afraid of Eyda.

Edmund at least spoke perfect English, but both he and his sister were incredible wimps. Ros was hopeless at the hopping game but she always beat Edmund who just didn't try. Catherine refused to play the game altogether, and any talk of running away – well, neither of them would even listen.

Ros couldn't talk to either Meee or Quintus and that only left Rhodri. The boy was full of spirit, fiercely proud of his tiny homeland of Gwynedd and Powys – an independent kingdom in his day. He would talk about anything, didn't seem afraid of Eyda or anything else, but Ros couldn't convince him that the mountain was almost finished. In any case he was quite sure there was nothing to be done. Maybe he was right.

It all came back to Eyda. If only Ros could find a way to change her mind. If she knew a bit more about the girl it might help.

This was the last bout of the night. Two more hours to supper and usually they sat around, sang songs and talked until the food came – the way it must have been for families once, before TV was invented. Ros gathered her courage. She couldn't forget that smile, that look in the Norse girl's eyes whenever she got angry, but there was no other way – not in this chamber anyway. Ros went to sit at her side.

If only she could get the girl alone without wretched Gwyn – if only! It was Gwyn now, not Catherine, who braided Eyda's hair each morning. He followed her everywhere and he was such a creep! He didn't have to *keep* complimenting her and agreeing with everything she said. The weirdest thing was that it wasn't creeping really – he meant every word.

'Tell me about – you know, what happened before,' Ros asked Eyda. 'How did you get here?'

The blonde girl smiled. 'When I am child, I live in Raumsdal in Vestland. When I am small – perhaps five years – Father hears of richer lands. Is great leader, Erik Bloodaxe – is sailing there to be a king. Father pledges to Erik and we come to Northumberland. There Erik is met with welcome and is made King of York.

'People there are lowlanders, southerners – you call Danes. Father is blacksmith. Is work and much money, but Father . . .' She shrugged. 'I remember little. Perhaps he doesn't like those lowlanders or perhaps . . . He wants son – what man does not? – but he has no son.'

She seemed wistful for a moment, then she grinned. 'Some great leader, Erik! Two years and he is driven out – without any fight. Another Norseman comes from Ireland—'

'Ireland!' said Ros.

'Yes, are Norse kings in Dublin, many many years. Now is trouble for us who come with Erik – but two years more, new king is gone and Erik returns. People welcome him again – crazy, crazy, who can tell with these lowlanders? Is more trouble of course. Now Mother is pregnant and Father hopes always. Before child is born she takes fever and dies.' A deeper shrug. 'Father loves me as his son. I try to be son for him – always I try.'

'Perhaps that's why you're such a good leader and all,' put in Gwyn, who was following every word.

Eyda shook her head. 'Those days women do many things, do *all* things. Is no greater leader in

Northlands than Asa, great-grandmother to Erik Bloodaxe. If Erik himself has half her strength—'

'Tell us about her, then,' said Gwyn. Oh, why couldn't he leave Ros to it? But he was totally hooked – the boy who couldn't sit through a history lesson without being told off for fidgeting.

'Is man called Gudrod, king of – oh, are many small kingdoms then.' Another shrug. 'Gudrod is neighbour to Asa's father. Both are kings. He wants Asa for wife, asks for her but father says no. Then Gudrod comes with army, kills everyone, takes Asa back with him.' Again Eyda grinned. 'How do you always say it, Adam? – are barbarous times back then. Now Asa bears son to Gudrod, but her mind is filled with her father's death . . .'

For a moment the blue eyes were far away. Then Eyda shook her head slightly. 'All men think Asa good queen to husband, but she waits her time, plans her revenge. Before child is one year old she kills Gudrod with her own hand. He has many kinsmen, Gudrod, but none dares oppose her, not a one – strong men, eh?' Eyda laughed.

'Well Asa finds new king, puts him in Gudrod's place, takes her son and goes back to her father's land.'

For a woman to do such things in such a barbarous place! Any other time Ros would have been as fascinated as Gwyn and the rest, but she had to bring things back to Eyda herself. If only she had the nerve to interrupt.

The Norse girl was telling that Queen Asa ruled her father's land for her son until he reached eighteen. By that time the country was strong enough to conquer all the other little kingdoms, so that the boy, named Halfdan the Black, became the first King of Norway.

'Then is Freydis Erik's-daughter,' Eyda went on. 'Great explorer, leads men to Vinland – is your America. This Freydis comes after me – a later time.' She gave Adam an odd smile. 'Is Adam's tale and *he* must tell. Yet are others. One is Aud the Deep-minded.'

She launched into a new story. Ros had lost her chance for now. Oh, what was the use?

There was one other hope – the last of all. Perhaps it would be better to leave it till tomorrow. But this was the perfect chance, while they were all sitting around Eyda, listening to her tales.

Ros got up, went over to the washing buckets,

then felt her way along the wall to the chamber entrance. There'd be other mining chambers, probably close by. Adam said there were but when she suggested going there to get help against the man in the slate mountain, he said it was too dangerous. And when she asked why, he just walked away as usual.

Ros stopped just inside the chamber entrance, looked back at the lights, the dim figures. It *was* safe here. So what was the danger out there — the flatfaces? If she turned back now, she'd never go.

She slipped out into the tunnel, turned right, and felt her way along the wall through the perfect darkness.

15

Ros stopped, listened. It had been dark like this when they'd first arrived in the mine – but then there'd been the sounds of others walking behind them and in front, and she'd had Doc's hand to hold.

Now she was alone – two steps along the passage and she couldn't even hear their voices any more.

The usual wimp stuff – heart pounding, burning in her eyes – but she *wasn't* going back. How had it looked out here? The wretched ring-lamps were always so dim and . . . There'd been other openings, on beyond their chamber – she'd passed them on the way to the mountain. There must be a line of work chambers along the seam of slate – did slate come in seams? If only she'd listened more carefully in that geography lesson.

She was just putting it off. Ros felt her way along the wall. The floor was smooth and level and the rock under her fingertips was like a friend. If she kept to this wall, she *couldn't* get lost. But what about the danger Adam had mentioned? The flatfaces needed lights. Surely she'd see them coming.

Her fingers found an opening and she stared in. Lights and voices, so this must be another work chamber. Should she call to them? Or – no, better to slip over there quietly, make sure it *was* a work chamber first.

Ros walked slowly towards the lights, very careful not to stumble. There were kids, sitting in a circle, just like in . . .

Someone grabbed her from behind, pulled her arms back. At her scream the kids jumped up, turned to face her as she was shoved forward into the light.

'What you doing, creeping in the dark?' A voice from behind her.

Ros tried to turn but her arms were jerked upwards. 'Please don't, I'm from the next – oh, *don't*!'

She looked around – no friendly faces here.

'Got no work here, so why you here? Why?' It was a boy who was holding her. 'Why no light?'

'I didn't want to . . . Stop hurting me! Let me go!' She tried to pull her arms free, kicked out behind her and her foot struck something. She was shoved forward. Other hands grasped her, turned her . . .

'No-one makes trouble here.'

Ros was held between two kids. Someone had hit her – she must have been half-stunned. A tall dark-haired boy – perhaps the chamber boss – was grinning at her. 'If you're lucky, I'll call flatfaces. If not . . .' He was trying to frighten her – surely he wouldn't . . .

Those threats Eyda had made when they arrived – in her own chamber, she could do anything at all. This boy's face was dark and thin – like Eyda, perhaps he came from a more cruel age.

'Please let me go.' Forget asking them for help. If only she could get back to her own chamber.

'Let her go.' A new voice, but it was soft and uncertain.

Ros looked around with the rest. Adam walked out of the darkness.

'Ha!' said the chamber boss, 'one more.'

'Sorry,' said Adam, 'she shouldn't have come. She's

new – she doesn't know. I'll take her back.'

'Why shouldn't I call flatfaces?' asked the boy. 'Give you both to them. Have some fun first.'

'You don't know how to call them,' said Adam. 'Anyway they wouldn't want to be bothered. Bosses are supposed to sort these things. *Her* boss will sort it when we get back. Don't make trouble – if Eyda loses people, she'll come looking.'

'A girl! What kind of crew has girl for boss? Get him!'

They moved towards Adam now and the dark-skinned boy didn't try to run, just let them take his arms.

'Forget them, Peter.' This was a tall girl with light reddish hair. 'Who wants trouble? I was enjoying your story. Let them go.'

The boss – Peter – came right up to Ros and closed his hands around her throat, while two others held her in place. Then he snorted. 'Shouldn't be here. Don't come back.' Suddenly they were released. Peter walked off and sat down. The other kids sat with him and ignored them.

Adam grabbed her hand and pulled her towards the chamber entrance.

'Thanks, Adam. I didn't—'

'Ssh, don't say anything. I'll handle Eyda.'

'Does she know—'

'Leave it to me.'

He led Ros back to the chamber, back to the circle. They sat down facing Eyda. The blonde girl stopped talking, looked Ros up and down, just as she had on the first day.

Adam met her gaze, shook his head slightly. Then he smiled.

'You never finished your story,' he said, 'about how you got here.'

Eyda stared on and Ros felt that fluttering of the heart again. Then the Norse girl smiled too, melting icicle fears to all the hope of spring.

'In York is more trouble – even more. Erik Bloodaxe has no hold there – Father says soon he falls again. For us is much danger. Father hears of other Norsemen living in west. We set out to find them, he and I alone. Is long journey, much happens on that road – I tell perhaps tomorrow. We come to mountains – you call Wales – hear again of Norsemen on sea coast to north, turn north to find them.

'Is evening.' Her voice was quieter all of a sudden. 'Wheel is lost from wagon so we stop to mend. With darkness, come robbers. Father is mighty man, has sword and spear ready, as any wise man. Yet those robbers have cowardly bow. They bring him down, then come and slit his throat.

'I take his sword but – Adam works out for me, says I am then twelve years – I cannot kill even one. I don't know why those men don't hurt me but they take me with them to mountains, mean to take me to their home.'

No wonder she'd been angry when Ros talked of tragedies the gods allow to happen – to see her father murdered in front of her . . .

'I am wild with grief. Then I think of Queen Asa. For revenge, I must be clever. So now I am gentle. I go with those robbers. When we stop for night, they don't tie me – a child, what can I do? What! I wait till all are sleeping, take knife from leader and kill him, then another, then another. Third one cries out and others wake. I cannot fight, so I run.' Eyda paused, staring at her feet. 'I run away, with revenge unfinished.' The lovely face was set now. The blue eyes shone, colder and brighter than ice.

'I wander that night, next day, see no man, no house. Another night – I am weary, lie down to sleep. Then I wake and moon is bright, see people: flatfaces and wagons and children. I am afraid of flatfaces, yes – but children go with them and I have nowhere else. I follow, come here.'

The fierce look came back into her eyes. 'One thing I regret – those who kill my father still live. In that world is evil, much evil. Here all live safe – I allow no trouble here.' She turned to Gwyn. 'Those robbers, they are of your race and Rhodri's, dark of hair and eyes. I do not forget. Is why I am hard to Rhodri sometimes. Is why I am hard to you.'

Gwyn snorted. 'You just did what you had to do, didn't you? I'm tough enough, I am – I know you wouldn't really hurt me.' He put a hand on her arm and Eyda smiled. 'You're right about one thing though,' the boy went on. 'With you in charge, this place is a hundred times better than anything you'd find out there.'

He meant every word! Gwyn was really happy here, doing the hard manual work, following this girl, clearly adoring her.

And he did have a point this time – Eyda was

absolute ruler here but she was good and kind and just. It *was* better – better than Llantri Comprehensive for a start.

The problem was that Ros had had her answer. There was no help in those other chambers and she'd never persuade Eyda. Only a week left and Rhodri was right. There was absolutely nothing to be done.

16

Eyda got up and left the circle, off to wash before supper.

There was one person Ros hadn't tried yet, and Gwyn was closer to Eyda than any of them. Why so hard to ask him? – it had even been easier to go out into that dark passageway. Oh, it was *stupid* – he was different in here and there'd never be a better chance. Ros swallowed hard, jumped up before he could leave.

'Gwyn, I need to talk to you.'

'Ah, Madam Rosalind.' He swept one of his bows.

'Don't do that *here*, Gwyn.'

The boy frowned. 'You're right,' he said at last.

'Eyda wouldn't like it, and anyway – well, you're not the same in here, are you? You've been pretty brave and I've got no reason to be mean to you.'

What reason did you ever have? – that was what she wanted to say, and what did he mean she 'wasn't the same'? Never mind.

She got one of the lamps, and led him off towards the workface. Whether *she'd* changed or not, Gwyn certainly had. That happened to bullies, didn't it? They met a bigger bully and it had this sort of effect. Of course Eyda wasn't a bully at all and so neither was Gwyn any more.

'Don't you think we should be doing something?' she asked him. 'Please don't say that Eyda doesn't think it's a good idea – and if you mention Redbeard, I'll scream.'

He didn't say anything.

'*She's* our Redbeard,' Ros went on. 'If we could just persuade her . . . Look, will you talk to her? If she'll listen to anyone . . .'

The boy was quiet a minute longer. 'I'll try if you like,' he said at last, 'but don't expect it to do any good, mind.'

Ros went back to the circle, found Adam waiting

for her. He led her into the hut and Doc followed.

'Where did you disappear to—' the smaller boy began.

'Tried another chamber – tell you later.' She just wanted to know what Adam would say.

'I don't know how to begin,' he said at last. 'I don't know why it's so hard either. You two – I knew there was something different. When you went off like that . . .'

'What do you mean, different?' asked Ros.

'All the time I've been here, no-one's even suggested running away, let alone doing something about the slate mountain. Why *is* that? Look at Rhodri. At the monastery he was safe, had good food, but he ran away – not because they were cruel or anything. I can't get him to complain about the place at all – except to say there was too much routine. He wants to please himself, Rhodri. He risked his life to leave that monastery but when I ask him why he doesn't try to leave *this* place – he doesn't *know*.

'And what about Eyda? When her father was killed she could have left her precious Redbeard to punish those robbers, but she's disappointed she didn't kill them *all*. Even if she *is* boss, she's still a prisoner here and someone like that isn't going to just accept captivity.

'Something's happened to us. I know I've changed. My father works for the Daiwa Bank. I had *everything*, and good friends, too. I have friends here – of course I do – but to just accept this simple life—'

'If we *are* different from the rest of you,' said Doc, 'why do you think that is, then?'

Adam shook his head. 'I'm not sure, but it may have to do with *when* you came here. Maybe they put something in the food and it takes time for the effect to build up – some drugs are like that. That boy – the one the flatfaces chased in here yesterday – *he'd* only just arrived. There's something even more important, though. Do you believe that one person can – well, make all the difference?'

'Yes.' Exactly what she'd just told Gwyn. 'You mean Eyda?'

'That story she wanted me to tell you, about Freydis Erik's-daughter—'

'We don't have time for stories, Adam.'

'Just listen. This Freydis went to Vinland twice – that's North America – the first expeditions there by

Europeans. On the first one she was pretty important and on the second she was the leader. They were attacked by the natives – they called them Skraelings and the historians think they were probably American Indians. The Vikings lost the battle and they were all running away, would probably have been massacred, but Freydis was pregnant, so she couldn't run. She picked up a sword from a man who'd been killed and chased the Indians off, all on her own!'

'That's crazy,' said Doc. 'How could one woman—'

'Well, it's a story from the Icelandic Sagas and they aren't considered very reliable,' Adam admitted. 'But the point is, when I told Eyda, *she* believed it. She *knows* one person can make a difference. She knows she can. And she never had the dream.'

'The dream – you mean that *everyone* had it?' asked Doc.

'Well, I can't ask Meee but everyone else – except Eyda. We were *chosen* for this, but why? – maybe because we're the sort who won't cause trouble? Maybe the dreams were a kind of probe to find out what we're like, to choose the docile ones. I think they're being doubly careful – first picking people who won't make trouble, then drugging the food or whatever to make extra sure. But Eyda never had the dream, and of course she wasn't brought here. She—'

He was interrupted by raised voices. Outside the hut two flatfaces were waiting and Edmund was clinging to his sister, both of them in tears.

Eyda separated them gently. 'Is time,' she said. 'Be brave.'

'You *can't* let them take him—' Ros began, but a glance from Eyda cut her off.

Edmund, who had always been as spineless as an average jellyfish, struggled so hard between the flatfaces that they had to use a pain button before they got him to the chamber entrance.

Ros turned to Eyda. 'How could you?'

'Is the way.' But the blue eyes were clouded and she didn't seem too happy about this part of the way at least.

'What's *wrong* with you? He was your friend. He depended on you. What do you think they'll do to him?' For Catherine's sake she shouldn't say this but she couldn't hold back. 'They might hurt him. They might do what they did to your father. Would you let them take your friend in that other world?'

The taller girl's eyes narrowed and her lips were tight. 'Here is not that other world. I say before – you don't help me, Ros, and still—'

'Right!' shouted Ros, too angry even to be sensible. 'OK, what do you think about this? When they were bringing us back from the slate mountain, I noticed that one of the flatfaces was a woman. So where do flatfaces come from, Eyda? I can guess, can't you? They're all tall, so they'd only pick the tallest kids. You're the oldest, the one they'll come for next, and you're tall, aren't you? How do *you* fancy it?' Ros put the flat of her hand against her own forehead, drew it sharply down in a gesture of cutting off her face.

Eyda was darkening but her eyes were bright. 'Go to bed now, Ros,' she said. 'You do not eat tonight. Go now!'

Poor Edmund – it was too much. Before Ros knew what she was doing, her hand came up and struck the taller girl across the cheek with all her force. 'You're a coward!' she shouted. 'You're not the one who took revenge on your father's murderers.'

Eyda stared at Ros a moment. Then she smiled her smile, the frozen smile, the exact same smile she'd smiled at Gwyn when they'd arrived here.

17

Eyda seized her arms with fingers that seemed strong enough to crush her bones. She marched Ros into the hut, pushed her down on to her bed in darkness. 'Stay here. I don't want to hurt you.' She was gone.

Oh no – she was going to throw up. Ros gagged, clenched her teeth, tried to stop her hands from shaking. The nausea passed and she buried her face in the pillow and cried – tears of anger more than fear. Poor Edmund – he'd always been so afraid. What were they doing to him now?

She lay in darkness. No chance of sleep so she'd have to lie here for more than ten hours. If only she wasn't such a coward. If only she could *make* them do something.

Ros heard the food arrive and a boy she didn't know came in with a ring-lamp to change Edmund's bed, which set her off crying again. Then there was a new commotion outside and someone else came into the hut – no light this time and it couldn't be sleeping shift yet. Whoever it was sat down on the next bed. A small hand found hers.

'Doc! But you shouldn't—'

'It's all right. She said I could come – seems a bit ashamed of herself, see. There's a new boy come, called George, from the nineteen-twenties. Adam's been talking to him, quiet like. He's all for escaping, or doing anything he can, so it looks like Adam's right, doesn't it? – about drugs in the food, I mean. Anyway, tomorrow George will go to the mountain and we'll get a better idea of how long—'

More noises outside – Eyda's angry voice. 'He just comes here. Now he eats his food. Then is sleeping shift. Come tomorrow.'

Soft words of reply – it must be the flatfaces, come to take the new boy to the slate mountain.

'Be swift then!' snapped Eyda. 'He misses sleep, he

will not work well tomorrow. Do not delay.'

Sleeping shift at last and in they all came – without the new boy so he couldn't be back yet. When everyone was in bed, Eyda turned off two of the lights and went outside to wait for him.

Catherine was crying. If only Ros could go to the girl and comfort her, but as usual she didn't dare. At last someone did go – it sounded like Rhodri. There were restless noises everywhere. No-one was asleep.

An eternity went by. Catherine was quiet, then Eyda brought the new boy in, a bit taller than Rhodri, slimmer and rather pale with sandy, almost blond hair. Eyda showed him to his bed.

'Sixty five,' he announced before lying down.

'Are you sure?' Adam's voice.

'Shhh,' said Eyda. 'All must be sleeping now.'

The boy lay down. For a minute there was silence.

'Oh, my God!' cried Doc.

Adam must have reached the end of his own calculation. 'It's tomorrow, isn't it?'

'I make it less than twenty hours,' said Doc. 'I don't see how we—'

'Quiet all! Is sleeping shift. Talk tomorrow.' Eyda's voice was cold as a winter sea. Her back was turned but the others could see her face and no-one spoke again. She stood for a moment, glancing around the hut.

'Men say this is my homeland,' she said, her voice much softer. 'Is a fool who lies awake all night, thinking of his problems. Morning comes, he is worn out and his troubles are same as before. Sleep now, all.' She didn't get into her own bed though – she went outside and turned out her lamp.

Another dark eternity went by and the Norse girl didn't return.

When it was time to get up, Eyda was grim as the slate-face and neither Doc nor Adam looked as though they'd slept at all. Both boys sat meekly at their breakfast bowls, not seeming to want to speak.

'So what's up then?' asked George, the new boy, at last.

Ros glanced at Eyda, swallowed down her fear with a mouthful of porridge. 'The slate mountain will be complete today. It will, won't it?' she asked Adam.

'I think so.' He looked at Doc. 'Some time during second shift, I think. I've been over and over it and

– your hundred and sixteen *was* correct?'

Doc just nodded.

'Listen, all,' said Eyda.

Ros couldn't stop herself flinching as the girl stood up, towering above them, just as she had when they arrived – feet apart, arms folded.

'Is no work today. Is enough slate piled.' She turned to Ros. 'I think that Redbeard sends you to me. Is Thialfi and not Redbeard who destroys the Mist Calf. I am not hero like Thialfi, yet . . . If abomination is complete today, we act now. Adam, what is best to do?'

No-one argued. Whatever Adam's strange force was that had kept them from revolt, these few words from Eyda swept it away. All the boys were keen. Catherine was white-faced and tight-lipped but her jaw was set. As for Meee, she couldn't have any idea what was happening but she was tense and eager – she must sense the excitement in the others.

Porridge bowls were cleared away – no-one was hungry any more.

'We have to get out,' said Adam, 'find – the police, I suppose.'

'How are we going to find our way, though?' asked Gwyn. 'It's like a maze out there.'

'I can,' said Doc.

'*What* – you can remember all those corridors?' asked Ros. Why hadn't he said so before? They could have . . .

'I remember things like that,' said Doc with utter confidence, 'but I don't think it will help in any case.'

'Why not?'

'When we were brought here, the children who came in with us weren't all from our time, were they? If we go back the way we came, where do you think we'll come out? Or rather, *when*? If we come out in prehistoric times, there won't be too many policemen around!'

'There won't be anyway,' said Adam. 'It was a stupid idea. Even if we end up in my time – or yours, Doc – the tunnel entrance is in the middle of the moors. Say we did get to a town, a bunch of kids wearing sacks and sandals – they'd never believe us. And what could they do anyway – a handful of policemen? We need the army – I suppose we do but . . . Actually, some of us have to try it, but it can't be our only plan. With so little time—'

'We have to go to the mountain,' said Doc.

'Some of us do,' Adam agreed, 'but there's sure to be trouble there. Doc, you're the only one—'

'Wait a minute,' Ros interrupted him. 'You want *us* to go to the mountain? If you think the police can't deal with it, what on earth can we—'

'Is no time!' snapped Eyda. 'We decide quickly – decide now.'

'Right,' said Adam. 'Doc – you're the only one who knows the way out. Go with Catherine. Try to get help.'

Catherine didn't want to go, for Edmund was here somewhere. They all started trying to persuade her and Ros was about to join in. But hang on a minute – *she* didn't want to go to the slate mountain, where the flatfaces would be waiting with their pain buttons. So why wasn't she volunteering to go with Doc?

No, she wasn't going back, no matter what anyone said. Whether they could actually do anything useful or not, Adam was right, it was their only hope and they had to try. She was the one who'd changed Eyda's mind and now she was going to see this through to the end, whatever it meant.

There was a light at the entrance to the chamber, coming closer. Too early for the washer-uppers – no-one should be coming in at this time. The children got up, formed a tight group behind Eyda. There were two lights and three flatfaces. The front one was a woman.

'Is there trouble here?' she asked.

18

'Is no trouble,' said Eyda imperiously. 'Why do you interrupt work?'

'You are not working,' replied the flatface woman.

'We're discussing work procedures,' said Adam quickly. 'Ways of doing things more efficiently.'

The woman turned slightly to Adam as he spoke, then back to Eyda. 'This will be reported.' They turned away, started across the chamber.

Eyda reacted instantly, jumped forward to punch the last of the flatfaces at the base of the neck. He went down, showed no signs of moving. The other two wheeled around. The woman held a pain button in her free hand, but Rhodri and Gwyn had moved with Eyda and they each grasped one of her wrists, twisting until both lamp and weapon were dropped. The other flatface moved towards Eyda but Meee was there too, driving her head into the sacking-covered midriff – just like in the hopping game. The man went down, clutching his stomach.

The two boys had the woman under control now and Eyda picked up the pain button from the floor. 'You take us to Slate Mountain.'

The woman didn't reply.

'You understand?'

Still no reply.

Eyda pressed the button against the woman's back and she screamed, convulsed, then slumped in the boys' grip.

'You take us to Slate Mountain,' Eyda repeated.

The flatface seemed to have recovered, but still she said nothing. Eyda used the pain button again.

'Stop it!' cried Ros.

Adam, with Meee and Quintus, was holding on to the other flatface on the ground. 'They won't help us, Eyda,' he said. 'Perhaps they can't.'

The blonde girl threw down the pain button, slammed her fist into the side of the woman's head, knocking her out, then moved on to the man, leaving him unconscious too.

'Somehow they know something,' said Adam, 'about what we're doing, I mean. Get the equipment. We can use the mallets and drilling rods as weapons.

'What about the gunpowder you use for blasting down the slate?' asked Gwyn. 'Maybe we could use that to blow up the mountain.'

'Other kids bring it, and set the charges,' replied Adam. 'I don't know where it's stored and anyway, none of us knows how to—'

'Look at this.' Doc had the pain button. 'You press here to work it, but there's a dial on the back as well.'

Gwyn took it from the smaller boy. 'I'll turn it up to maximum – no telling how many flatfaces we may run into out there.' He twisted the dial and a pale yellow spot at the centre swelled to a glowing disk of red.

'Come on,' urged Adam. 'Forget the gunpowder. Doc and Catherine go back for help and Eyda will lead the rest of us to the mountain. We'll find that guy and—'

'I can't,' said Doc.

'Can't what?' asked Ros.

'I can't go back, can I? I bet you no-one but me knows the way to the mountain either.'

Adam turned to George. 'You were there last night. Can you remember the way?'

The boy shook his head. 'I wasn't paying much attention. I'm sorry.'

'I know!' cried Ros. 'Doc can draw us a map.'

'But there's no paper,' said Gwyn.

'We can use slate – like they used to in schools. Rhodri, can you get Quintus to split off a flat piece? How much do you need, Doc?'

The three boys went off to the slate pile, came back with a lump about twenty centimetres square and a centimetre thick. Doc set to work at once using a rock splinter as a pen.

'Hurry!' said Adam, standing over him.

Ros pulled the boy away. 'If he makes one mistake, we'll never find the place.'

'You're right. Come on, Eyda, let's get some other kids to help us. We don't know how many flatfaces there are out there.'

They left Doc scratching away, with Gwyn, Meee and Catherine to keep an eye on the unconscious flatfaces. Eyda strode into the next chamber before Ros could stop her – of course, she didn't know that Ros and Adam had been here last night. She went straight over to one of the two cutting parties.

'Stop work!' she shouted. 'All come here.'

The dark-haired chamber boss – Peter, was it? – came rushing over. 'You should not be in here. Go back to your own chamber.'

'All listen to me,' said Eyda.

The boy was as big as she was and his face twisted in anger. By now his entire crew had arrived and Eyda's party was surrounded. 'I'm boss here,' said the boy. '*You* will listen to *me*. Get them!'

Ros was grabbed from behind, tried to twist free but lost her footing. Whoever was holding her fell with her, clawing at her neck. Everyone was shouting and pushing and someone stumbled backwards on top of Ros, pinning her to the floor. In a minute she'd be crushed.

Then there was a scream of agony.

19

'Stop fighting! All listen to me!' Eyda's voice, then another dreadful cry, as though someone was being murdered.

Ros was released and managed to drag herself out of the scrum. Eyda was standing with her back to the workface, holding the chamber boss around the neck, and twisting his arm behind him. She wrenched it up and the boy screamed for a third time.

Everyone was watching. It was ten against six, but with their leader helpless these kids didn't seem to want to fight any more.

'Tell them to listen to me,' commanded Eyda.

'Yes, yes, listen,' gasped the boy.

'Today Slate Mountain is complete,' Eyda told them. 'I do not permit this. We stop it. All, bring tools and follow.'

They looked at their chamber boss, who was clearly terrified.

'Yes, do what she says.'

A short dark-haired girl spoke up at once. 'It's no use, Peter. We can't change the system.'

'Yes, we can!' This was the tall red-haired girl who had helped Ros and Adam the night before. 'What about the October Revolution?'

'What's that?' asked the first girl.

'Is no time for talk,' said Eyda. 'Pick up tools and follow.' She set off towards the entrance, hauling the chamber boss along with her.

No-one picked up anything and no-one followed.

'We can't,' said a boy half hidden in shadows at the back. 'Is not . . . Can't, is all.'

Eyda stopped and turned back. Adam pointed at the red-haired girl. 'You just arrived? Will you come with us?'

'Thirty shifts ago.' She came to stand beside him. 'Yes, I'll go.'

'Before that, who came last?'

The boy in the shadows spoke up. He'd been here two hundred shifts and there was no way he was going anywhere with anyone.

'It's no use, Eyda,' said Adam. 'They don't know you like we do. We're just wasting time.'

Eyda released the dark-haired boy and pushed him so that he stumbled to the ground. 'Take lights then,' she ordered.

'Leave one,' said Ros. 'Don't leave them in the dark.'

The ring-lamps were collected without resistance. Eyda shook her head, tossed one of them back to the chamber boss, then led the way out again.

They tried two more chambers, got four more ring-lamps but no recruits at all.

'This is taking too long,' said Adam. 'We've got enough lamps for everyone. Let's see how Doc's getting on.'

Back in the chamber the small boy was hunched over the block of slate, still scratching away. 'Two minutes,' he said, without looking up.

'What worries me,' said Gwyn, 'is, even if we destroy the mountain or that wizard fellow – well, what happens to us then?'

'There's no alternative anyway,' said Adam. 'If the mountain is completed and the world turns into what we saw from the top — well, it wasn't *my* idea of paradise, for sure.'

'Done it!' shouted Doc.

The map was clear enough, a twisting line, bristling with small dashes where all the other passages led off. The only other things he'd marked were the place where the strange light shone down and the exit to the slate mountain bridge.

'Is very good, Doc,' said Eyda. 'You two go swiftly now — Redbeard protects you, I know it.' She clasped their hands in turn, Catherine pale and trembling, Doc as calm as ever.

Ros gave the little boy a hug, then Gwyn clapped him on the shoulder and winked. 'No problem, Doc,' he said. 'You guys will be back with the SAS before we have a chance to do anything.'

And off they went, with Doc leading the way.

'What about these three?' Adam pointed to the flatfaces.

'They must not raise alarm,' said Eyda. She knelt down, lifted the woman against her knees, took hold of a shoulder with one hand and the half-head with the other. She was going to break her neck.

'Stop!' screamed Ros. 'You don't have to kill them.'

Eyda looked up at her, let go of the woman and shrugged. 'I say before – they must not raise alarm.'

'Oh, please, you can't. Please leave them.'

'Come on, Eyda,' said Gwyn. 'They'll be out for ages after you hit them like that.'

Eyda stared at them a moment longer. Then she set the limp body back on the floor and stood up. 'I do not understand.' She looked at Ros. 'If you wish it. We go then.' She grabbed one of the ring-lamps and led the way to the chamber entrance.

Ros picked up Doc's piece of slate and followed – there was bound to be more trouble with the flatfaces and having the map was the best possible excuse for keeping well clear of it.

There were nine of them, with a lamp each. Gwyn had the pain button and the rest were carrying mallets or drilling rods, except for Meee who didn't seem to want one, and Eyda, who hardly needed a weapon.

Ros caught up with the Norse girl. 'I've got the

map – I'd better lead.' Eyda smiled and waved her past.

At first the passage was straight with regularly spaced openings in the right-hand wall, probably the entrances to more work chambers. Then it turned to the left and there were lights – at least ten flatfaces waiting for them. Suddenly all the kids were rushing past, brandishing their weapons.

Ros stayed by the corner. If she lost her place on the map, they'd never find the way. Of course the real reason was that she was terrified – couldn't bear the thought of being hurt, or of hitting someone else, not even a flatface. With Doc and the Tudor children gone, it looked as though she was the only wimp left.

The kids were on the attack at once, swinging their rods and mallets. Some of the flatfaces had pain buttons, perhaps they all did, but they couldn't get close enough to use them. Two of them went down and the rest were retreating. The only kid in trouble was Meee, flat on her back and resisting with all her surprising strength, while a flatface tried to force his pain button down on to her chest.

Ros went as close as she dared. She ought to help,

but all she had was the map and she couldn't risk breaking it. She could kick the man but . . . Meee twisted her head towards the sacking-covered arm and her jaws clamped. The flatface screamed, dropped the pain button and then there was blood everywhere, spurting from his arm. He released the girl, grabbed the wound and staggered off along the corridor, taking a blow on the shoulder from Rhodri's mallet as he went.

For a moment Ros was unsteady on her feet and she turned quickly away to the neutral rock of the passage wall. She'd known the flatfaces were real people, not robots, but to see that blood – now she *really* knew. She shook her head to clear it, looked around and it was over – all the flatfaces were down or gone, apart from one, still grappling with Eyda. Gwyn came up behind the man, his pain button glowing red. There was a sizzling sound, flames burst from the sacking and Gwyn jumped back as the flatface crumpled at Eyda's feet.

Adam went to look, gasped, 'He's dead!'

Gwyn dropped the pain button, then stooped down, white-faced, to get it back. 'I'd better turn this down a bit.'

Ros fought another wave of dizziness, turned away from the body and the blood, but the smell – just like that time Mum burned the sausages . . . Just ahead of her, Rhodri picked up another discarded pain button. With a fierce grin, he twisted it to maximum. This boy had lived in a more savage time. Like Eyda he might well have seen men killed, and who could ever tell what Meee had seen? She stood beside Eyda, face and hair and arm and smock spattered with red. Ros had never seen the tangle-haired girl smile, but now her eyes were bright and there was a small twitching at the corners of her mouth.

'Lead on,' said Eyda and they started down the corridor again.

They passed turning after turning, junction after junction – no-one to bar their way and the map was perfect. Doc must have a photographic memory – he'd never told her that. No wonder he remembered every word of every book he'd ever read.

Almost there! The final turning was visible ahead. No more branches after that, just a short length of corridor, the stairway up to the entrance and . . .

Ros came around the corner and stopped. There

were no branches, but ten metres ahead the tunnel ended in a blank rock wall.

20

The tunnel ahead was dead straight. There were no intersections, nothing but bare rock.

Eyda turned on Ros, cheeks flushed. 'You lead us wrong!'

Familiar itching burned in her eyes. How *could* she have let them down? Seeing that man killed and all that blood, maybe . . .

'Leave her alone, Eyda,' said Adam. 'The map might be wrong. Let's go back. If we can get back to our chamber, at least we'll know where we are.'

Something was wrong. Doc had drawn it all to scale, every turn and every side-passage perfect. The map *must* be right. She *couldn't* have misread it. So why . . .

'Do as Adam says,' declared Eyda. 'We go back.'

'What's this?' It was the red-haired girl – Ros still didn't know her name, or when she came from. She was half way down the dead-end passage, staring at the side wall.

Eyda went to look and Ros grabbed Adam's arm. 'The map *isn't* wrong. Look, we came round this corner and – see this arrow Doc's drawn, this is where that funny light was – exactly where the passage ends down there.'

'Come on.' Adam went to join the two girls and Ros followed to find a small circular depression in the side wall.

'So what?' asked Gwyn.

'It could be a lock,' said Adam, 'and we've got something that fits. Gwyn, try it, but turn it down first.'

'I already have.' He stepped forward and placed his pain button into the depression. It fitted perfectly.

Gwyn hesitated, then pressed. Cracks appeared in the side wall. A door swung back, then chaos: flatfaces rushing out, the children swinging their mallets and rods. Someone shoved Ros back into the far wall of the passage, jarring the map from her hand. They didn't really need it now but still she scrabbled after the lump of slate – it was her only excuse to keep out of the fight.

Ros got hold of the map and looked up. Eyda and Gwyn were driving for the door shoulder to shoulder, with Rhodri and Meee right behind them. There weren't so many flatfaces out here now. Quintus and the red-haired girl swung their weapons, chasing them off down the corridor.

Ros followed the rest into the midst of chaos, shouts and screams, the air reeking of burned clothing and singed flesh. She shrank against the wall as Quintus and the red-haired girl came in, then stepped back into the doorway. At least she could keep a lookout. One of the flatfaces pushed past her, ran off down the corridor.

'Let them go!' screamed Ros. 'They're trying to escape.'

Across the chamber Eyda held one of the sack-clad figures pinned against the wall, but another came behind her, pain button outstretched and glowing red.

'Eyda, look out!' Ros jumped forward but she'd never make it in time.

Then someone else hurtled in, between Eyda and the weapon. It was Gwyn. The flatface crashed into him, there was a scream and both went down. But Gwyn lay still, while the man struggled to his knees. Ros kicked him as hard as she could, but her foot caught his thigh, doing no damage at all, and the man rose to his feet.

Eyda was still busy with the other flatface and Ros shrank back against the chamber wall. The man stood over her, pain button ready, then, perhaps seeing a chance to escape, he darted across the chamber and out through the door.

A minute more and it was over. The four flatfaces in the room all lay motionless. Gwyn was still down, with Eyda crouching over him, while the rest of the kids crowded together on the far side of the room.

This wasn't a bare rock chamber like every other place they had been. It was some kind of a control room. In front of the far wall was a sloping plastic desk, with switches and . . .

Eyda roared – more the sound of a wild animal in pain than any human voice. 'Is dead!' she cried. 'He saves me and he is—'

'Let me see.' Adam prised her away, grabbed for

Gwyn's wrist, then his temple. 'No heartbeat – just a chance . . .' He picked up a pain button, turned it down low, shoved it under the taller boy's smock and held it to his chest above the heart.

Gwyn's body convulsed. Then he was moving, coughing, raising a feeble hand.

'This one is hurt also,' shouted Rhodri.

It was the red-haired girl, the burn-mark of a pain button on the right side of her ribs. Adam worked on her for minutes, then stood up, shaking his head. 'I can't . . . we . . . have to go on,' he stammered.

He stood up, face very pale, lips tight, and walked over towards the controls. He was leaving the girl. She must be dead.

'The end of that passage out there – it's some kind of a door,' said Adam, his voice steadier again. 'Maybe this will open it.'

Ros thrust down horror and nausea and went to stand beside him. If they fell apart now, it would all be for nothing. That girl would have *died* for nothing.

There were several rows of switches set into the panel face, as well as two large knobs with graduated dials and, on the right hand side, a big yellow lever.

The plastic surface had marks which must be writing but it made no sense.

'This must be for setting it, I suppose.' Adam's face twisted with doubt. 'Maybe the big switch will open the door.' He closed his eyes, winced as he pulled it.

Nothing happened.

Ros dashed out to the passage. Where the blank end wall had been, the cold pale light was shining down. 'Come on, it's open!'

'I will not leave him.' Eyda clasped Gwyn tighter still.

'I'm all right.' Gwyn's eyes were open and he struggled weakly. 'Go on. I'll follow.'

Ros saw her chance. 'You go on, Eyda. I'll help him.' A new excuse to keep out of danger. With the bigger girl's help she got Gwyn to his feet and found she could support him with an arm around his waist.

'Go *on*, will you!' cried Gwyn, and Eyda led the rest off through the eerie light.

At the other side it was just as before. Not much farther, but Gwyn could hardly walk and Ros struggled to keep him upright. Ahead of them the light seemed dimmer than it had been last time. As they reached the steps, Rhodri came back down –

helped her haul Gwyn up to the start of the slender bridge.

It *was* dimmer but somehow it was clearer than before. The sky was grim and heavy with a deep sulphurous tinge – not cloud because the moon was up, a couple of days past full. The colour of it made her look away – a sickening brownish purple.

Suddenly the ground trembled underfoot, the air was full of thunder and everything was lit as bright as noon. Ros looked up to the summit of Slate Mountain where twin pillars of fire roared up to the heavens, as bright and fierce as rocket jets. Shielding her face against the light she saw that the pyramid shape was perfect now. On its pinnacle a figure stood, dressed in a long dark robe. His arms reached up above his head and those colossal shafts of naked power were rising from his outstretched hands.

'He's completed it already,' shouted Ros. 'We're too late!'

21

Above them, the lord of Slate Mountain lit the world with the power of his creation. Below, the dark mist swirled all around the pyramid, rising up towards them, seething with those unnatural and sickening lights. Ros looked away – anywhere but there. Eyda was saying something but her words were lost in the roaring from the pillars of fire.

The Norse girl turned to face them.

'Is too dangerous.' This time her voice was powerful enough to pierce the tumult. 'All others stay here,' she commanded. 'Is alone up there. I go up and kill him.'

'Wait!' cried Adam. 'Eyda, listen, get them back to

the control room. Quickly – don't leave anyone behind.' He sprinted away into the tunnel mouth.

Eyda stood a moment, turned again to stare up at the figure on the mountain top. Then she grabbed Gwyn around the waist and pulled his arm around her shoulders. 'All follow Adam, quick.' She hauled the injured boy off down the steps with the rest at her heels.

Ros went into the control room, keeping her eyes from the pale still body of that brave, brave girl whose name she'd never even known. She went to stand at Adam's side in front of the control desk.

'This must be . . .' The dark-skinned boy hesitated. 'That funny door out there and all these things with time . . . It's possible that these controls change *when* you go to – the time on the other side of the door, I mean. Maybe we can get to the mountain earlier, before he has the chance to . . .' His voice trailed off and he stood staring at the panel.

Eyda was right behind him, her face darkening, mouth twisting to a frown. Rhodri's hands tightened on the mallet, while Meee shifted from foot to foot, like a little kid who needs to go.

'Why do you do nothing?' demanded the Norse girl.

'Because I don't *know*!' Adam wheeled around to shout into her face – he'd never been like this. 'If I pick the wrong control, *anything* might—'

'What anything? What happens then?' Eyda demanded.

'I told you, I don't know.'

'You call me back from mountain.' Eyda hadn't been this angry, not even when Ros provoked her. 'If you can't—'

'Better close the door first anyway,' said Ros quietly.

Adam took a deep breath, and pushed the yellow lever back. 'Yes, I'm sorry. Rhodri, can you check the door, then keep a lookout, please?'

The Welsh boy went out to the corridor. 'There's no light now. The passage is a dead end again.'

'So now . . .' Again Adam hesitated. 'Time's continuous, so it's more likely the dials than the switches, but which dial? We don't know what the other one does. We don't *know* what *either* of them does. Oh, I wish Doc was here!'

Ros glanced at Eyda's face, quickly put a hand on

Adam's arm. 'You can't be sure,' she said. 'Just try one.'

'Do it now!' commanded Eyda, clamping a firmer hand on the boy's other shoulder.

Adam reached for the top dial as though it was red hot, turned it a tiny fraction anti-clockwise.

'More!' demanded Eyda.

'No! We don't know . . .'

Ros pulled the big lever. 'Let's go back and see.'

'It's open again,' shouted Rhodri from outside.

Eyda led the way out and the rest followed, Gwyn walking by himself now, still shaky but recovering fast. Back through the light, back to the tunnel entrance and Slate Mountain.

It was exactly as before, the sulphur sky, the purple moon – but no, surely the moon was a bit lower than it had been.

'You've done it!' cried Ros. There were no columns of fire, no figure up there and the peak of the pyramid – hard to see from here but . . . 'It's not finished – I'm sure it's not!'

Eyda ran across the bridge and up the pyramid stair with the others trailing behind her. That darker place, near the stair-head must be the opening to the pyramid's heart. People were pouring out and swarming down towards them.

Ros went up as fast as she could. Only Gwyn and George were behind her, but no-one was that far ahead. Weapons swung – another battle. She'd have to be extra careful – one slip here and . . . Even as she reached them, Rhodri hit a flatface with his mallet and the man lost his footing and rolled out of sight below.

Most of the flatfaces had backed out of range on to the narrow ledges beside the stair. A gap opened ahead and Ros dashed through, twenty more steps, less. She reached the opening, the other stair leading to the chamber inside the pyramid, peered down into the empty darkness, then went on up towards the top. One block missing, only one, and two children struggled up over the far edge carrying that final block between them.

'Place it now!' There was no mistaking that voice – the owner of Slate Mountain. But where was he?

'Stop!' Ros forced herself on, heart hammering from the climb. 'Don't do it!' The kids didn't hear her, or they weren't listening. She was too late. They were about to set the block in place.

Something Doc had said – or Adam – about the shape and mass of the pyramid having to be exactly right.

Exactly.

The kids lowered their burden. Ros found something in her hand – the map! – and threw it. The lump of slate bounced once, skipped on under the final block just as the kids set it down. Ros rushed on to look. The pinnacle block was off-centre, tilted slightly to one side, and its surface was giving off faint wisps of dark smoke.

Everything was suddenly brighter, as though someone had turned on an electric light. Ros looked up, found shimmering brightness in the air itself. There was a small noise behind her and she wheeled around. The two children had gone but the man from the mountain's heart was standing there, shrouded in cloak and hood as before. She gasped, took a step back, and came up against something – a wall! The two of them were inside a glowing bell which covered the peak of Slate Mountain. It was woven of tiny dancing strands of light, like those which had played from the creature's finger ends before, but these were much paler, much thinner.

Ros shoved her weight against the light-tent. The wall gave a little but it was stronger than canvas – she'd never break through.

'It is ruined.' The cold soft voice. 'My mountain is ruined and soon it will melt down. But we have time.'

'Time for what?' Ros edged around the light-wall to get as far away from him as possible.

'*This* mountain is ruined.' He sounded more amused than angry. 'That does not matter. I will make another. It will take centuries, in the years of your world, but your centuries do not matter to my people. They can wait a little longer for their home to be complete. And you – you are the one who has destroyed my mountain. You will help me build the new one.'

'Keep away! I'll never help you.'

'My servants are lost with my mountain. You are younger and smaller, yet you will be the first of the new ones.'

Ice flooded arms, legs and fingers as she realised. 'Servants – you mean the flatfaces?'

The creature made a gurgling noise, a little like laughter. Hands came up to throw back the hood.

His neck was scrawny as a chicken's and the head was bald, skin so pale it was almost white. But the front, where the face should be, was mirror-flat, mirror-smooth, mirror-bright. He came straight towards her and Ros saw her own face reflected there.

She screamed and tried to dodge, but an arm shot out, a bony white hand took her by the wrist. There was something in his other hand now, a small wriggling caterpillar of darkness. He held it up between forefinger and thumb for her to see.

'When this is put inside your head it will show you what you must do, but first . . .' He put the thing away, came out with something else.

Ros pulled and struggled, screamed for help, but she couldn't break the creature's grip. Even if she did get loose, there was no way out of the light-tent. He was showing her something else now – hard to tell what it was at first. There was a handle and a flat shimmering thing that must be made of light. The shape was like the blade of a butcher's cleaver.

Ros screamed as she realised what the thing must be, kicked out at the folds of the creature's robe, struggled even harder.

With another gurgling laugh, he pulled her closer. 'So ugly, all of you. I do not need to remove these faces of yours, but why should I live surrounded by such ugliness? One simple cut – here.'

He raised the light-blade, set it flat against Ros's chest and brought the edge of it up under her chin.

22

His arm was tight around her, clamping Ros's head down against his knobbly shoulder as he prepared to make the cut.

She screamed and screamed for help, still struggling, stamping and kicking at him, trying to prise the arm away. Ros couldn't see the light-blade now but she felt it tingling against her throat. Then he stopped, let the weapon fall away. Over on the far side, the wall of the light-tent was bulging inwards.

The owner of Slate Mountain was staring at the place – at least his mirror-face was turned that way. The bulge was growing, with the shapes of hands shoving at the outside. Then the light-tent disintegrated to a cloud of swirling fading fragments which showered Ros's hair and shoulders, lighter than the finest snow.

Eyda was standing there, face flushed and twisted with exertion. At once she smiled her icy smile.

'I don't know if you are Loki, Mischief-maker,' she said. 'Whoever you are, Redbeard sends me for you.' She said something else, perhaps in her own language, and strode forward.

The robed one shoved Ros aside and whirled his hands above his head, wreathing himself in strands of lightning. He cast a shimmering net, snaring the Norse girl in a basket-prison of light, then stood with arms outstretched towards her.

Eyda had her arms out too, trying to force a way forward to get at him but the net was stronger than the light-tent had been. Her face twisted as though she was carrying the whole mountain on her shoulders, and as Ros watched, the Norse girl went down slowly to her knees.

No time for cowardice now, no time even for thought. Ros threw herself forward, beating at the robed figure with fists, lashing out with her feet. It was like kicking metal railings. Under the robe, he seemed impossibly thin, but her blows had no effect at all.

Ros felt a sudden pain like an electric shock, found herself thrown back to the edge of the mountain top. She almost went over, then steadied herself. Perhaps her attack had done some good after all because Eyda was on her feet again, closer to her enemy and, inch by inch, forcing her way closer still.

Their fingertips touched and Eyda's light-prison exploded into a fountain of sparks, like a whole box of fireworks going off at once. Ros was blinded, looked away, then back to see the two struggling together. The creature had the light-knife in his hand again, but his arm was gripped by both of Eyda's hands, brought down across the girl's thigh. There was a sound like green wood snapping, the knife bounced away over the edge and the arm flapped around as though it was broken.

The robed figure pulled free, tried to get past Eyda to the stair. The girl grabbed handfuls of the robe, yanking him back, almost ripping the garment away, leaving him sprawled across the smoking pinnacle stone.

Ros had a brief glimpse of limbs and body, very

pale and impossibly thin. Then Eyda was on to him again, grasping him around the waist. She heaved him up, took a couple of steps and, with a twist of her powerful body, threw him off the edge.

There was a sharp cry, a splintering impact and the shattered ruins of their enemy tumbled out of sight down the mountainside.

Smoke was rising from the surface of all the blocks now and the air was warm, almost stifling. The blocks themselves were hot – hot enough to feel through sandal soles. He'd said the mountain would melt down – it would be like Doc had said, like an accident in a nuclear reactor . . .

Eyda took a step towards Ros, crumpled to her knees, shook her head. 'Is not Loki. I do not know . . .'

It was getting hotter all the time – like standing in a furnace mouth. Eyda looked about to collapse. Ros started towards her but the Norse girl clenched her fists, came up to her feet again.

Adam was here too, now. 'Look down there! There's grass and trees.'

Above, the sky was dark blue, the moon a silver ghost, and that must be the east, where a bright red-yellow sun was rising. But the heat was unbearable. Ros fought black waves of giddiness, clutched at someone for support and found Gwyn helping her this time. The grey smoke rolled down like water, shrouding the sides of the pyramid, but farther below a dull red glow was swelling.

There was a crash as the bridge which had joined the pyramid to the hillside fell to shattered fragments.

'We'll have to go inside the pyramid!' screamed Adam. 'The slate is melting out here.'

He led the way to the opening and on to the stair leading down to Slate Mountain's heart. Gwyn bundled Ros along behind him – it *was* cooler in here. She felt better at once, shook free of the Welsh boy and stopped to count the others past. They had been nine with the red-haired girl, then eight and, thank goodness, all eight were here. Ros followed them to the bottom of the stair and along the corridor into the cubical chamber.

'What happened up there?' Adam was standing beside her.

Ros told him about the slate map, the last stone out of alignment. 'He was going to . . .' She retched as she remembered the light-blade against her throat, the grip of that bony arm. She just *couldn't* tell him about that. 'Eyda came and threw him down.'

'Well done, Ros,' Adam said softly. 'Everything's changing back to normal. The Life Energy must be releasing itself. I think – I think we must have done it.'

'We have. The mountain's ruined – he told me that – but if it's . . . He said it's going to melt down. How are we going to get out of here?'

'Is nothing here, Adam.' Eyda arrived before the boy could answer. 'We searched all. No door, no lock, nothing. What now?'

Adam was quiet a moment, eyes down, face screwed up in concentration. 'I don't know,' he said at last. 'I don't think . . . Oh, I'm glad we stopped that guy, but . . . We're trapped in here. There's nothing we can do.'

23

Adam had never been close to crying but now he turned away and dashed a sleeve across his face.

Meee cried out – the first sound Ros had ever heard her make.

She hadn't been hurt – at least there was nothing to see – more as if she was terrified. 'Meee, meee,' she cried and cuddled into Eyda's arms, clinging on as though she wanted to break the Norse girl's back.

Something was happening, something weird – she was blurring, fading. Then, all in a moment, she was gone, leaving Eyda clutching at the air.

The tall girl turned on Adam, face dark and twisted. '*What is this?*'

'I only hope, if everything is being restored — perhaps the energy has sent her back.'

'What about Edmund?' shouted Ros. 'What about Doc and Catherine and that poor brave girl?'

Adam's cheeks were damp but he smiled. 'I don't know. I'm only guessing but it won't hurt to believe they'll all be all right now. Maybe Meee was first because she's the oldest — in time, I mean. Rhodri, you'd better explain all this to Quintus, because if I'm right, he's next.'

It was getting hotter in here — not as bad as outside, not yet, but even if Adam was right, would they all get out of here before they roasted? Eyda didn't seem to notice the heat. She was grim-faced, staring at the dark slate floor. After a while Quintus spoke quietly to Rhodri.

'He feels — he can't explain — something he has not felt before,' the boy translated.

Eyda held the Roman boy as she had Meee, until he was gone. She smiled fiercely, knowing she would be next, embraced them each in turn, first George, then Rhodri, then Adam. 'Thank you for your wisdom,' she told the boy from the future.

She came to Ros next and held her close — again

it brought the wretched tears. Eyda wasn't crying. She looked almost triumphant as she released her grip. 'I don't know if Redbeard sends you, yet . . . Once I say you don't help me, Ros, but I am blind then. You do more than help – teach me so much. You it is who shows me my destiny. I am fortunate to know you.'

Ros struggled to reply but words wouldn't come through the tears.

Eyda went on to Gwyn, held him close, as she had the others, then kissed him on the mouth. 'Brave warrior, you save my life. I wish with all my heart that you come with me.'

'Do you think I don't!' Gwyn was crying now.

Eyda hugged him again, stepped back from them all, struck her pose, feet apart, arms folded on her chest, face set as hard as any slate. 'Listen all,' she said. 'Another thing Father tells me, a saying of our folk: When I am young, I walk alone and I lose my way. I know myself rich now, when I find my friends.' Her eyes fell on each of them in turn. 'Man's joy is in man.'

A moment later. 'I am ready.'

It began. Then she was gone.

'Oh, Adam,' sobbed Ros. 'What will happen? Will she go back – you know – to the moors and . . . Those robbers might be waiting.'

'Hah,' said Gwyn, 'if they find her, it's them that I feel sorry for.'

Adam shook his head. 'I don't understand this any better than you, but . . .' Suddenly he was grinning. 'You know that story, the one about Freydis Erik's-daughter? Eyda is short for Freydis and her father was called Erik too, so that's her name. She told me, if she ever got back to her own time, she would *be* that Freydis – how she wanted to see the New World.

'It was good for her to have something to hope for. I didn't have the heart to tell her that *that* Freydis was the daughter of Erik the Red, the Viking leader who colonised Greenland.'

'You said the stories aren't that reliable,' said Ros. 'Could Freydis have been Erik the Red's daughter-in-law, or adopted?'

Adam laughed out loud now. 'More than likely,' he said, 'but one thing's for sure. Eyda was born about 940. Erik the Red wasn't even born then and the Vinland expeditions were seventy years later. No, she can't be that Freydis, but she knows that world well enough. There are lots of places she can go – the Vikings went *everywhere*. Of all people, she'll find a life for herself.'

The others said their farewells. Rhodri was gone, then George.

By this time it was at least as hot as it had been on the mountain top – hotter – and there was a light in the passageway outside. Ros went to the chamber door to look. Down the far end, the walls of the corridor were starting to glow red.

'Will we be in time?' she asked Adam. 'I can hardly breathe.'

He was quite calm still, managed another smile. 'There's nothing we can do but wait. Oh, I hope Doc and Catherine will be OK, too. Eyda was right – such good friends, all of us.'

'Without you, Adam . . .'

He laughed now. 'I didn't do much. It was you two, and Doc – and Eyda, of course.'

Ros felt a cold tingling somewhere in her chest. This must be it!

'Please,' she said and grabbed Gwyn's hand – if only they could go together. 'I'm frightened.'

'And you think I'm not?' Gwyn smiled at her.

'Oh, Adam!' she shouted.

The boy from the future was smiling too but he was blurring and fading now, just as the others had. His lips moved – barely audible – something like, 'I'll be OK, plenty of time still.'

The room at the slate mountain's heart was fading with Adam, but Gwyn was here, his hand solid as ever in her own. A minute more and . . .

'It's freezing!' cried the boy.

24

It *was* cold, dark too – why hadn't they brought the ring-lamps? Not *that* dark though. Ahead lay moorland, oddly pale. There was a crescent sliver of moon and the sky was washed with grey, so dawn couldn't be far away.

'Snow, that is,' said Gwyn. Yes, there was a dusting of icing-sugar powder all across the heather tops. 'We don't usually get snow before November.'

Behind them was a steep hillside and a tunnel opening but it barely went back two metres, then ended in bare rock.

'Is this where we went in?' asked Ros.

'Look!' cried Gwyn. 'There's a light. There's a house down there, see?'

'What's this?' Something huddled at the back corner of the opening.

Gwyn came to investigate. 'It's Doc! Hey, Doc, wake up.' He was shaking the figure – too dim to see much.

'Sleepy,' came a fuddled voice. 'L'me sleep.'

'Come on, he's freezing. We've got to get him down to that house.'

They made a two-handed seat for the smaller boy, and set off across the frozen moor. Ros hardly noticed the snow-dust melting on her bare toes. Her mind was full of Eyda. If she had taught the Norse girl something, how much more had *she* learned. Her own problems: a new school, a bit of bullying – they had made her miserable enough but . . . Adam was right, Eyda would make a life anywhere, whatever problems she faced. Well, so would Ros! No wonder Gwyn thought she'd changed. Half the problems at Llantri had come from her expecting these Welsh kids to be the same as her friends in Sussex. Why blame *them* when she hadn't even *tried* to fit in? From now on things would be different.

They came into the yard of what must be a farm. Ros's hands were clasping Gwyn's, supporting the sleeping Doc. Whatever happened, she had two friends now.

'That's funny,' said Gwyn. 'At that window – it's a Christmas tree!'

No mistaking a Christmas tree. They *could* have one with all the decorations and flashing lights in the middle of October, but it would be deeply weird and farmers are supposed to be practical people.

'You know what this means,' said Ros, 'what it *might* mean?'

'What?'

'Suppose it *is* Christmas. All those funny things with time – it could be. We were in that place for almost five days. If it's Christmas now—' this kind of calculation she could handle, '—then more than seventy days have passed out here – fifteen times as long. Suppose it's the same for Eyda!'

Gwyn's hand gripped tighter on hers. 'She was there for three years, if Adam's right,' he said, 'and he usually is.'

'Multiply by fifteen – that's forty five years. When they sail to Vinland, she'll be about . . . twenty five.'

'And that means she'll have about ten years to get herself over to Greenland or wherever that Erik the Red lives and get herself adopted or whatever, before setting out!'

They reached the door, set Doc on his feet, supporting him between them. Ros knocked.

'What's happening?' Doc demanded. 'Where are we?'

'It's OK. We'll soon be home.'

The boy relaxed, about to fall asleep again.

The door opened – a tall woman in slippers and a long dressing gown. The smell of frying bacon washed out into the dawn, so at least they hadn't woken her up. She just stared at them.

'This is going to sound an awfully funny question,' said Gwyn, 'but can you tell me where this is, please, and what the date is?'

The woman's eyes widened. She hesitated, then Welsh hill farmer's common sense took over. 'It's Five Hands Farm, near Newydd. You'd better come inside.'

'That's not five kilometres down the road from Llantri,' said Gwyn, lowering Doc into one of the kitchen chairs.

'Is that where you're from, then?' the woman asked.

'Please,' asked Ros, 'what's the date – and the year?'

'You have to be joking! Oh well, it's Christmas morning, 1998. Now you kids have got some explaining to do. First of all . . .'

Ros turned to Gwyn, but she saw nothing but Eyda, a Viking helmet on her head and a sword in her hand, standing in the prow of a dragon-ship, her long fair hair streaming behind her.

Ros began to laugh out loud at the sheer joy of it.

She caught Gwyn's eye and the two of them laughed together.

NOTE FROM THE AUTHOR

***Fancy knowing more about some of the things in
this book?***

For the story of the ridiculous Mist Calf, the
altogether more serious giant, Hrungnir, and all kinds
of other crazy tales, try reading *The Penguin Book of
Norse Myths* by Kevin Crossley-Holland.

For more on the Vinland expeditions (and to find
out exactly how Freydis managed to chase away a
horde of Skraelings single-handed) read *The Vinland
Sagas*, translated by Magnusson and Palsson, in the
Penguin Classics series.

The children mined their slate in almost exactly the
same way it was done in North Wales 100 years ago.
To see a mining chamber just like Eyda's, visit
Llechwedd Slate Caverns in Blaenau Ffestiniog
(where the idea for this book was born) – or else
contact them and they'll send you all sorts of
information through the post.

Another Hodder Children's book

THE FALCON'S QUEST

John Smirthwaite

The city is under attack from barbarians' arrows, while a scheming prince is determined to undermine the Emperor . . .

A poisoner works under cover of darkness – and a competition between killer falcons has everything at stake . . .

Young Ping He is the only boy in his village to have tamed a falcon. Together, they brave ridicule and overcome treachery. Now they face their biggest adventure yet . . .

A Fidler Award winning novel